MW00815002

BLOOD A COLD BLUE

April, 2016

BLOOD A COLD BLUE

April, Well met at AWP!
Enjoy these strange tales.
Sláinte.

STORIES

JAMES CLAFFEY

Press 53

Winston-Salem

Press 53, LLC
PO Box 30314
Winston-Salem, NC 27130

First Edition

Copyright © 2013 by James Claffey

All rights reserved, including the right of reproduction in
whole or in part in any form except in the case of brief quotations embodied
in critical articles or reviews. For permission, contact author at
editor@Press53.com, or at the address above.

Cover design by Kevin Morgan Watson

Cover art, "Bird in Snow" Copyright © 2013
by Þorkell Sigvaldason, used by permission of the artist.

Author photo by Maureen Foley

Quotation from *The Red Tent*, by Anita Diamant (St. Martin's Press, © 1997),
in the story "Battle," used by permission of the author.

This is a work of fiction. Names, characters, places, and incidents
are products of the author's imagination or are used fictionally.
Any resemblance to actual events, locales, or persons,
living or dead, is entirely coincidental.

Printed on acid-free paper
ISBN 978-1-935708-91-9

for Maureen, my forever sea

Hold to the now, the here, through which all future plunges to the past.

—James Joyce, *Ulysses*

ACKNOWLEDGMENTS

The author wishes to thank the editors of the following publications where these stories first appeared:

Apocrypha & Abstractions, "Silenced by a Widowmaker,"
Artichoke Haircut, "Sixteen Magpies"
Bad Penny Review, "Where's Me Dinner, Woman?"
Bartleby Snopes, "The Night the Lights Went Out"
The Bicycle Review, "Ireland in Four Acts"
Blue Fifth Review, "Green Their Dead Eyes," "Losing My Voice," "Green
  Their Dead Eyes"
Bong is Bard, "Valvic"
Cease Cows, "Illuminating Every Fear"
Cobalt Review, "Bolt the Door"
Connotation Press, "Body Parts," "Privilege," "Santa Fe, NM"
Drunk Monkeys, "Spoon-fed Saliva," "Liver Spots"
Elimae, "The Green Hairstreak's Death"
Everydayotherthings, "Beloved Go with God"
Extract(s), "Thread of Red Cheesecloth"
Far Enough East, "Not Enough"
Flash Frontier, "Demon"
FWriction: review, "Kidney Trouble"
Gesture Magazine, "Nylon Folds of Oldness," "The Ribboned Corpse
  Cold"
Houston & Nomadic Voices Magazine, "Hellfire"
Jet Fuel Review, "The Blow"
The Linnet's Wings, "Bed-making"
Literary Orphans, "Still Life" (as "A Nod Is as Good as a Wink to a
  Blind Man")
Litro Magazine, "Splintered"
Metazen, "Her Shoulder an Enigma," "The Depths of the Steel Vault"
Molotov Cocktail, "The Way Her Neck Angled," "Bedwetter," "Sepsis"
  (part 3 of "Ireland in Four Parts"), "My Mother's Hands"
Necessary Fiction, "Birdcage," "We Sank My Mother's Mother"
Negative Suck, "Autumn Tinged with Mud"
New Orleans Review, "Skull of a Sheep"
Pithead Chapel, "All This Lifelong Later"
Prick of the Spindle, "Roadkill"
Prime Number Magazine, "Jam Jar"

Pure Slush Real Anthology, "Spreading from the False Fly"

Red Fez, "Witness for the Prosecution," "Orwell Lodge Hotel, Room No. 8"

Revival Literary Journal. "Cold Hands"

Santa Fe Literary Review, "The Bitter Light of the Single Bulb"

Spittoon 2.3, "Gardenia & Tarot," "Tattoo"

Thrice, "Headache," "The Cane Flays Bare"

Thumbnail Magazine, "Childbirth," "Mercury Retrograde"

Thunderclap Press, "Brooklyn, NY"

Toronto Quarterly, "Tell My Wife I'm Sorry"

Tuck Magazine, "Holy Communion"

Unshod Quills, "Fryday, June 17th, in the Year 1681"

Up the Staircase, "Bingo Night," "Avocado Grove in Six Movements" (winner of the Up the Staircase Challenge: Place)

The View from Here, "Fragments of the Bird"

Word Riot, "Blood a Cold Blue"

BLOOD A COLD BLUE

BLOOD A COLD BLUE

Inside my head the cracked shells of ochre-tinged crawfish litter the place. At night, I wear a knit cap to keep the shards from falling out and staining the pillow. More than my fear of dirty pillowcases, I fear discovering the contents of my mind. Not one to complain, my love will take the orange-hued mess in stride. Maybe the stains remind her of the ginger-haired boys she was drawn to in her teens and early twenties? One had translucent pale skin, and a tattoo of a WWII sea mine on his shoulder blade. How do I know this? I find myself crawling in her dreams on nights when I have little to amuse myself, save the task of counting the crawfish in my own skull.

I collect the lint from my navel in a small jar we found by the banks of the Liffey. One day, I hope to weave it all into a catgut replacement, so I can string my tennis racquet and take to the courts again. I run drills for hours each morning, the force with which I strike the ball with surgical precision is fearsome. I have 0% body fat, despite the pizza I eat from the Onion Field, and the two Clancy sisters who work there—angels, both—comment on my thinness. The younger one, Helen, is a bratty schoolgirl; a real smart-ass, with a pixie-like quality that makes me sweat whenever I see her. She will trade her pixiness for a cast-iron puritanism that forces her family to send her to a clinic on the Beara peninsula for six weeks. When she comes back home it is with a seagull's head where her own lovely one used be. We meet on the 46A to Dun Laoghaire one day. Me on the way to a tennis tournament in Greystones; her seeking the brine of the coastal air. As the bus trampolines up and down I touch her neck, right where the short afterfeathers fluff outward.

The curved metal of the seatback on the bus is cold and her feathers remind me that we are not the same, that we cannot, and do not, and shall not be together, no matter how much I want for us to fall in love and live happily ever after. Her school coat is threadbare at the elbows and the burgundy sweater pokes through. My head fills with rattling, the bus driver going too fast and the green-blue water to the left blurs and changes into a vast sheet of plastic. I know how many are in my skull, the dead bodies collected in a pile in the center of the floor. The scab on my knuckle from where I skinned it on the coal shed lock hangs like a hinged potato crisp. "Can we feed the birds on the pier?" I ask—immediately regretting my question. One pin feather on her nape bristles and I examine my dirty fingernails.

Stained-glass windows. The sun in blue, in green, in red. Jesus falls a third time. In the shadow of the confession box we sit close, her thigh against mine, her pinkie touching mine. Love is sacred, love is a dream, some form of penance for thinking we might work out in the end. My words are knots, tied fisherman's, stumbling to be said. She kneels on the pull-down cushion, joins her hands. *O clement, O loving.* The rain-stained pavement leads us to the sea, where we shall search for winkles, valvular shells, the coursing of the corpses in my head. Shimmer, simmer, the seashells summon the answer from her silent lips. I love the fragile feathers, the way she turns her head to look at me, her clear black eyes, the sharp beak, and how the tubercule sits within the nare, as if a pearl trapped in an oyster.

In a box under my bed I keep one of her feathers. I also keep a black hair scrunchie I found in her coat pocket. When I dream of her she changes from one to the other, her feathers melting into red, into luster. I steal her nail polish, the foam-green one, and with the door jammed shut, I paint my toes and the thrill ripples through me like the time I put my wet hand on the lightswitch. Holding her hand on the road to the pier, the sun hits her nails and my secret is safe. I want to paint her toenails, too. Then we can be the same, only different. Would she allow me to put one in my mouth and suck on it like a Kola Kube? Her hands are paler than snow, the blood a cold blue layer beneath the skin. On a garden gate a thrush perches on a silver fleur-de-lis. The breeze brings salt water mortal sin.

THE GREEN HAIRSTREAK'S DEATH

His mother sleeps beside him, the heat coming off his damp pajamas, the steady burr of her snores falling through the broken floorboards to the empty lounge. Out back in the yard the bantam and hens roost in the branches of the destroyed apple tree.

In the dream, his mother's mother is in the butcher's shop of a strange town, in slippered feet, her nightgown in flitters. "A pork chop and a nice slice of liver while you're at it," she says to the ruddy-faced butcher. He takes her hand and places it on the cutting board. He drizzles sawdust over her mottled skin and cleaves the hand off from the wrist. A ribbon of butterflies, green hairstreak, dingy skipper, and brimstone stream from the wrist and flutter off. The butcher wraps the still limb in brown paper, tying a double knot with thick twine and says, "That'll be tuppence ha'penny." The old woman tries to take the package, but more and more butterflies spill into the air and everything turns to black.

His mother kneads handfuls of creamy dough with orange-stained fingers. Nicotine addicted, persecuted, her day is a maddening circle of tea and biscuits, baking, smoking, the necessary fiction of the housewife. Yellow rubber gloves and the tin of Vim; she heads for the outside toilet, her wedding ring nestled in the soap dish on the

kitchen window ledge. He left a log floating in the bowl—
a perch—bound for open water. The apron hitched about
her waist, the filth enough to send her into hysterics. In
matters of the household she is the senior partner, the one
who fishes the lump out of the fell water and quickly bags
it, her cigarette smoldering in the narrow hut. Does it matter,
she wonders, the flecks of tomato seeds in the water, the
rusting bones of the old Morris Minor in the yard?

The Paperwhites fold in the weak evening sun and a fool
crosses the street in the shadow of the primary school. In
the crib, baby gums its fist, patterns of saliva stain the sheet,
and the hole in her stocking worries itself ever larger. She
puts another briquette on the fire, knocking the dust off
against the coal scuttle. Her dirty hands are the direct success
of a hard life, the creep of years, the baby a latecomer.
Through the curtained window the dusk moves along—a
boat on a slow-flowing sea.

Mother told her as much—how she'd be marrying a
moocher, one of the shiftless kings of the small town they'll
be forced to quit in disgrace when the banks close the taps
on the loan and the bailiffs cart everything off to the
Showgrounds for auction. Made of stronger mettle, she
drops the bottle in the saucepan of water and lets it bubble
away, all the while reading the pages of last night's dream.

On the stove the bottle rattles against the side of the
saucepan and she takes it out of the boiling water with a
dishcloth. She squirts a drop onto the inside of her wrist to
gauge the temperature and crosses the kitchen floor to the
crib. Outside, a mackerel sky, she watches a single green
hairstreak settle on a dandelion, and the memory of her
mother's stumped wrist sends a sharp pain shooting across
her forehead. Baby smacks the rubber nipple and the mint-
colored creature flies into the window, as if trying to say
something with its death.

COLD HANDS

We are two ends of a magnet pushing in opposite directions, the idea of anything between us, a silly one. Even when I steal a bottle of wine from the off-licence in town, so we can sit on the sea wall at Sandymount, and watch the gulls veer in the wind, it is an ill-thought-out moment.

We amble the streets; you pea-coated and snug in worsted, and me in an old Belstaff anorak, teeth chattering. The time we see that strange bird with the curved beak and carrot-colored feet? We thought it a castaway from one of the oil tankers out at sea, a lost soul marooned on our stretch of sand, a disabled dove thrown from its nest.

I am glad to be with you. The rain doesn't bother me like it does you, and your poor hands, iron deficient, blue in the winter days. But we are playing at love, imagining a future that cannot ever be. When we embrace that first time under the snow-topped wall, your lips taste of peppermint.

Research shows that peppermint increases memory, and even now, thirty years after that kiss, the faint scent of menthol lingers. My boss wears a peppermint-scented perfume sometimes. I smelled it on her when we were out by the estuary the other day and I flashed back to nuzzling your neck under the fuchsia bushes.

The horn fastener from your coat is still on my desk—a prop from an old story—the only link to you I have left. Even now, the memory of your quiet breathing excites me; those afternoons when we snuck into your house and fell asleep in your bedroom, the rain tapping the windows, your hands and feet cold as death.

SILENCED BY A WIDOWMAKER

A pretty way to die, crushed by the falling limb of a giant eucalyptus tree. The morning started out okay—a hot shower, the gardenia-scented bodywash, soaping between her legs, the tickle of flowing water, a popcorn kernel trapped between the front teeth. From the upstairs window she could see the trees by the path that runs to the cliffs. Fog misted the window and she drew a happy face, the same way she'd done in her parents' car when she was a little girl; her hot breath on cold glass. She ran her fingers through her silky hair, slick with conditioner, and thought how she was still pretty, in an unconventional way.

The buzzer of his flat door didn't sound right the previous night when she'd pressed the button and held it down. It sizzled, she thought, like there was a loose wire, or something. A lifeguard, he drove a 50s Chevrolet truck with whitewall tires. Fate, he decreed, the night they met. Dirty martinis and stuffed olives, an art fundraiser for the local high school. His son would have been a senior had he lived. A flutter rippled through her when he leaned over and asked her what she thought of a small still life of a rum bottle and bag of onions. She was able to read the 120% proof label on the bottle. At least it was "authentic," she told him.

They sat at the back of the truck, their feet dangling, passing a bottle of red wine back and forth. They kissed with a feverish intensity. He said he was nervous, years since he'd done this with anyone. His wife left after the accident. Moved to Memphis to be close to her mother. She took the cat, too. That hurt, he said. His son had named the pet, Mr. Bones. Because it was all "skin and bones," he added.

The argument had been a bitter one. His drinking, her insistence on condoms, their shared tragedies not allowing them to forgive. She wouldn't beg him to stay, not ever. "No one's putting a gun to your head," she told him. In the shower the salt tears mixed with hot water and far in the distance she saw his son struck by the falling tree-limb, over and over, until there was nothing but the pale bark of the eucalyptus and the dark feathers of the turkey vultures littering the ground.

THE WAY HER NECK ANGLED

In the tall grass at the perimeter of the field, a snail unglues itself from a stone and silvers its way toward a fencepost. My teeth chatter from the cold, the edge of my left eye twitches faster than my heartbeat, and there's a hollow feeling in the roof of my mouth. I am about to float away, to attach myself to a group of helium balloons and take to the air forever. But, instead, I am strolling towards the fire on the other side of the field, and my girlfriend remains behind.

Had she not made a joke about my time in prison I might have let her go, but the laugh out of her, the snide remark about loneliness, what could I do? The way she pitched forward and struck her head against the root of the stumped tree, the gash turned white for the longest time, and then the blood welled like blotting paper soaking up ink. I knew she was dead from the way her neck angled, the pale skin, her cigarettes on the ground beside her—Marlboro Lites—and me having told her over and over that smoking kills.

I know what my lawyer will say when he finds out about this one—twin to a left-handed simpleton—over his plate of tomato soup in the tony restaurant on Bleecker Street. Too bad, I think it's my inability to sleep that causes me to react so sharply. If only I was able to get a good eight hours and awake refreshed, I'd be a new man, and no mistake. The sparks from the fire shoot crimson shards into the night sky and across the field her body temperature lowers for the last time.

THE BITTER LIGHT OF THE SINGLE BULB

I don't know how she got there from the graveyard, but there was a bumping and a rattling in the boot of the car on the way home. The bones awoke at night and my heart fluttered, but a guttering candle on the bedside table protected me from all evil. Running the gauntlet to the toilet in the dark meant finding a way past the loose boards and the possibility of being caught and dragged under like a drowning victim. No lifeguard stood sentinel on the landing, only the bitter light of the single bulb—40 watt—flat shadows cast to the walls.

Chairs bore teeth marks, the foot of the piano stool slowly wore away until it rocked so precariously the tinkers took it away on their horse and cart. The horse struggled to pull the wagon away from the footpath and the old tinker with the porkpie hat angled on his head flicked the horse's rump with a bamboo switch. "Hup, yeh gluepotted bastard," he said, and tipped the hat towards us as the cart rumbled off and turned skilfully in the lane opposite our house. He must have seen me peering at him, because he spat on the road and said, "What are yeh looking at yeh wee pansy-boy?" I turned around and ran for the safety of the house, where Mam had taped several wooden tea-chests shut with black insulating tape from the Old Man's toolbox.

We'd lived in the house for ages. Ever since the Old Man had to leave his old hometown behind. He often spoke of missing the landscape of the Midlands, the wide spaces of the Bog of Allen and the giant turf-cutting machines, the fairy hills where at night the creatures came out to cause mischief and dance in the moonlight, and the whitewashed cottages and houses of the town with their meticulously-kept windows. His health slowly deteriorated—fingers curled from the arthritis, despite the ancient potato in his pocket to ward off such maladies—so they decided to sell the house, to downsize, and move closer to the country, closer to the stark graveyard on the hillside in Horseleap.

When the house sold, the next-door cat peed all over the couch in the sitting room, proof positive of the unsettled nature of felines. We spent days cleaning floors, soaping walls, removing the grease of ten-thousand fried breakfasts, and in our feverish state we ignored the increasingly hostile sounds from under the upstairs' floorboards. The moving truck bulged with headboards and mattresses, dining tables and mahogany chairs, grandfather clocks and armchairs, and when the buzzer sounded to lift the last load to the truck, we stood in the stripped-naked house and allowed the memories to wash over us like flowing silky sheets.

Part of me wanted to stay, for the forgotten treasures buried in the back garden: the toy gun with the faux-pearl handle, the Dinky Batmobile stuck in a cinderblock, the biscuit tin with the skeleton of the hamster inadvertently buried alive, the skeleton I drew on the side of the coal shed with leftover paint from when we painted the garden shed last year, the fireworks we'd bought from the sellers in Moore Street. The greater part of me wanted to escape, to leave the ghost behind, praying the Holy Water we sprinkled on the landing would be enough to restrain her restless soul. Before shutting the door for the last time and driving to the new house in the countryside, I climbed the bare staircase to the landing and in a last act of selfish charity slipped the Old Jamaica Rum 'n' Raisin chocolate bar between the cracks of the floorboards.

The Old Man locked the front door and pushed the key through the brass letterbox, the solicitor already having given the new owners their keys. The red-bricked walls seemed to draw him in on himself, as if he were shrinking in front of our eyes. He bent down and peered in at the empty hall for a moment. "It's the old dog for the hard road, I suppose," he said, and took Mam's hand, steering her toward the silver-painted gate. The linen curtains waved slightly in the upstairs window, even though the window frame was shut tight. Whether it was the late-evening sun playing tricks on the eyes, I could swear I saw a liver-spotted hand with its long fingernails waving at us from the window.

HELLFIRE

Smoke spirals from the Hellfire Club on top of the Dublin Mountains. Magpies like broken chessboard mosaics chatter in the trees. The Old Man turns the change in his pocket and the jingle rings in my ears. Mam is in the kitchen, making brown bread. The serrated knife cuts a cross into wet dough. The rasp of the striking match interrupts my reading and cigarette ash festoons the unbaked loaf. Desmond Brennan from next door fumbles his key in the Yale lock, his aged parents deaf and alone in their parlor. His bowler hat shines. The sun falls. Across the road, a small child pulls a pot of boiling water from a stove. From the bookcase in my bedroom I take out *The Collected Poems of Robert Frost* and transport myself to a New England landscape, the birch trees swaying in the breeze, and my Old Man asleep in his favorite chair by the hearth.

BODY PARTS

Skin—how it fades, falls, pitches, and finally collapses on the body. Silver in black, the needle in the stack. Time created this ill use, ionized water liberally taken, the promise of rebirth, of a tightening of stretched parchment, the bone written on in faint lines. A scar at the base of the big thumb on the right hand, bottled glass broken in bits on a cemented wall. Nothing remains visible of the original wound covered now by the cross on father's grave. Beneath the skin, part the sinews and tendons, his rotting body lies asunder.

Bone—marrowed lengths of knotted pain, the wingspan of a balsa-wood airplane, sent flying off the Hill of Tara, the old High Kings beneath the sod. The topography of the land is borne out on the frame of my body, the empty skeleton inside. In the shade of the enchanted forest a spider picks at the faded scar, its eight legs tickle the bone and jar the memories. The spiraling sycamore seeds remind me of home and the patterns hidden in the peeling wallpaper that grows old in lonely rooms.

Eyes—passed from father to son and back again, flecks of gold the only increase, a settlement of coin impossible. Strange how the sounds and the stares rebound, words fallen to the ground, the love held in place like a wired-shut jaw. And over time the surfeit of misery collects in the interstitial spaces between bone and muscle. One day soon, those griefs will be tapped by the fingers of a faith healer as he identifies meridians and unhappiness, pressure points and inhospitability. Until then the old negatives curl and fade, the worsted suits go threadbare, and the compass of the past shudders.

HOLY COMMUNION

Coats buttoned to the top, collar turned up against the east wind. The seagulls revolt against the beating rain and head for the shelter of the frothing Irish Sea. We march to the front door, the letter box opening and closing in the breeze, and single file we make our way to the church at the crossing points of Leicester Avenue and Rathgar Road.

On wooden beams the body hangs—thorn-crowned—a terrifying magnificence—the bloodied side real enough to dip your fingers in if you were close enough. In the echoing body of the church rules are followed or ears get clipped. The Old Man speaks of "civility," and nods to neighbors, known and unknown, brothers in Christ. Coughs, sniffles, the rustle of the Sunday newspapers, the altar decorated with the flowers of the season, lilies, white and stately.

In the pews there's not much room to budge. We kneel and rise, rise and kneel, mouth the memorized prayers and wait for the magic to unfold. Three rings: the host, a white moon aloft, the water into wine, transubstantiation. The Old Man says, "I am not worthy to receive you..."

I wipe my nose on a coat sleeve, silvered snail trail, and his eye half-warns me to "buck up." Two lines form, like the Russian bread queues, and the perfumed and powdered old ladies creep towards their savior. Bareheaded husbands, widowers, and bachelors ripe with age like soft peaches, shuffle altarwards. The Old Man rises to join the line and motions for me to do the same. I shake my head, mumble, "Not fasting," and his glare promises a cutting of the switch and the lowering of the boom when we get home.

I pick at the brass plaque on the bench in front, *In Loving Memory of Gerard McHugh.* Through the gap in the seat a handbag rests on the polished wood. As the congregation kneels and the host melts in wined mouths, my fingers reach out and pluck two half-crowns from the coin purse in a side-pocket. The sun breaks through the enormous stained-glass window above the altar, bathing the priest in a shimmering light. He blesses us for Mass's end and sends us forth to love and serve the Lord.

On the walk back we pass the big houses on Garville Avenue where the rich people live. Trees as big as giants fill the front gardens and the Old Man shakes his head and says, "All that matters is your health and your family." I know he's lying because he never stops talking about how we used to have more money than "any of these feckers." In the kitchen spooning cream of mushroom soup into our mouths, I finger the ridges of the half-crown and move my fingertips over the raised head of the British lion, thinking we may not be rich anymore, but I'll be able to buy whatever I want at the sweet shop later.

KIDNEY TROUBLE

The silver wheels of my misshapen kidney no longer work. The doctor diagnoses a problem with my spine, too. Mother's eyes are puffy and she dabs at her shrinking tears. They help position me in the hospital bed, my body lighter now than before, the boy I was, ripped from the present and replaced with some shrimp-like version of a weaker self.

He would be here, too, if it weren't for the drinking. She says if she had a gun she'd shoot him, but I know she's not serious. Serious is the blood in my urine. Serious is the rubber sheets I sleep on. Serious is the possibility I'll enter the gates of Heaven before either of my parents. In any case, she kisses me and tells me everything's going to be all right.

While the doctor ties a rubber tube around my arm to take blood, his knuckle grazes my cheek and the skin is rough. The thin steel needle penetrates my vein and I grab hold of the bedsheet and grit my teeth. A plant sits in a terracotta pot on the window ledge and the sun strikes the plastic leaves as the glass tube fills with dark blood. My tonsils are missing and if I open my mouth to scream he'll be able to see my stomach in terrible knots.

His hands trace the outline of my kidney and when he pushes in suddenly, it rattles. *Not a good sign*, he says. *Extended stay*, the doctor tells us. *A month. Maybe longer.* I want to go home, to sleep in my own room, with my soccer posters and stuffed bears. The doctor insists. He calls it *acute nephritis*. He says I'll have to be restrained at night. I don't know what he means, but when the nurse ties the straps around the bed frame I begin to shake and she gives me the magpie-eye.

Mother returns with my pajamas, toiletries, and a bundle of comics. The nurse brings me a slice of gammon ham with a pineapple ring and mashed potatoes for my tea. Mother kisses me and says she's got to go home to get Dad's tea ready, but I'm not to worry because he'll be in to see me after work. As she walks toward the glass double doors of the ward, I open a comic and try to forget my broken parts.

Dad arrives later with the other fathers visiting their sick children. Raincoats and the evening newspapers and the smell of damp and cigarettes make me want to get sick. He ruffles my hair and says I'm to be a good soldier for the doctors and nurses. His thick fingers feel like lead weights on my head and he gently kisses my cheek. After he goes home for his tea I cry into the pillow for a while.

In the darkness of the ward the faint click of shoes on tile mingles with the breathing of the patients. I dream of capturing insects in jam jars by the banks of the river, my skin wet with sweat from the rubber sheets. I'm woken twice during the night by the metal knocking coming from my kidney. The noise reminds me of the way the corrugated iron roof of the garden shed flaps on a windy day. I mimic the sound: *ehhhh, ehhhh, ehhhh.*

As the clicking of nurse's shoes draws nearer I hush up and press the pillow to my side so she won't hear my kidney's metallic groans. Maybe it's the pressure of the pillow, but I piss my pants and my pee spreads daffodil yellow on the bed and smells awful. I can feel the shape of my kidney through the skin and how it vibrates from the broken pieces.

THE BLOW

Here is the hand that dealt the blow that ended the marriage that created the baby that cried 'til morning that ate the sun that cudgeled the moon that battered the stars that presented the light to the darkened forest where the old woman slept when filled with her misery that created the hole that housed her heart that filled the cavity that breathed so shallow that she appeared quite dead and stirred so silently the caged bird cracked a caraway seed that lay on the floor from the day she left and changed the locks and shredded his clothes and drained the wine bottles and cursed his fine name as his child kick her ribs and pressed on her pelvis as she rode the bus that crossed the city so full of iron bridges and fish bubbling answers to the questions she had about the man she loved who dropped her to the floor and kicked the shards under the table that shook in the quiet as the garage door closed.

THE CANE FLAYS BARE

Church bells disturb morning, bubble down waterfalls of stone. Chapters of unmitigated grayness, celestial bodies moving through time, the point of a ballet slipper touching polished wood. The river billows over polished rocks, natterjacks in trees, dirty gray clouds streaking steepled sky, snow turned to slush in a musical interlude. The stonemasons' guild shut forever, next-door to the hardware shop. In a classroom they learn Punic wars and juried decisions, the tin can filled with pennies for curses uttered on the playground. Bother yourself, leave the others alone. Words of wisdom, the bangs, the bells, the falling bodies, fingers and toes counted repeatedly. Three touches and you must pass the ball. Bundled coats are goalposts, a game of skill, as John O'Connor flakes the ball towards the goal, his thick curled hair unmoved by the east wind. Small boy grits his teeth as the master swishes bamboo arsewards. The way the man hikes his sleeves up, thick, knotted arms—three cheers for savagery and prayers of mercy wordlessly muttered to a tin god. The first blow, a bluff, the hand stayed. On the second, the cane flays bare skin and cries from small lips chime.

IRELAND IN FOUR ACTS

1

Three brass pawnbroker's balls hang above a shop door on Lower Clanbrassil Street.

Leopold Bloom lived at number fifty-two.

The junction of Patrick Street, Dean Street, New Street, and Kevin Street was known as the "four corners of hell" because a public house used stand on each corner.

A large white swastika was emblazoned on the side of a brick chimney on the Shelbourne Road.

White swans floated serene on the waters of the Grand Canal at Portobello Bridge.

Street vendors cried, "App-ells, three a penny! Get yer lovely app-ells!"

Old ladies pushed prams with polished fruit and paper-wrapped flowers to their spots on Moore Street.

The Premier Dairies Milk Trolley drove down our road every morning before 7 a.m.

The rattle of the glass bottles sometimes woke me before Mam's voice called up the stairs.

2

An office with two chairs. A book read. A tray of animal crackers. Fracture no fracture. No voice. Vocal. Speak up, out, distressed. A cabin in Sligo, brass tub, the shining carapace of an old typewriter. Vote for meaning, tap the ampersand, allow the double-printed remains of a letter to flail on the page. Thin white paper never works. Keys cut "o"uts into the paper, a Holy mess. Stress the first syllable here, amalgamate the story with another, remove the ambiguous nature of the mystery character in Chapter 4 and replace with terms of peace treaty. Sneaking away from the chaos of the everyday seems wise. Main square, tall plinth, hatted man. Does the brass shine enough to cast a glow? Talk about what matters, expose the beams and rafters of the soul and curl fetal on floor. Cry, cringe. Allow the wash to cover you. Laugh cry same time different moment no matter no how no shame no knowledge. See the long fur coat and the double bass in its case the strings frayed and rotted. A place where only you go to find comfort. Lie in the basement of the wardrobe covered with a hill of bear a fossilized child a frozen tableau. Doors shut shimmer windows catch tongues cook daggers in old pots and the switch on the kitchen wall echoed and reverberated shock when hands were wet thrown across room and float accusations at the family. Dry your hands in future. Wash my hands of the lot of you. A refrain from the Book of Common Prayer.

3

Nurse holds my arm steady, the stitched scar raised, swollen and angry, red tinges around the sutures. Mam's worried face is about to melt like a Dali clock, into misery and blame. I have to be a brave soldier, she says, putting a cold hand on the knobbly knee beneath the flannel material of my trousers.

Silver, pointed, a-glint in the artificial lights of the clinic, the tip breaks the surface of the scar tissue. From the welled area comes the bloody pus, soaked up with gauze the nurse gently wipes about the crusted edge. A cry breaks from my lips, and Mam's eyes, behind horn-rimmed glasses, well with salted pity for her little soldier.

"Can I have the zoo animals?" We are walking along Liffey Street and Mam takes me into Hector Grey's Emporium of Imported Goods to choose a toy for bravery. There's hardly room in the small room to move. Tea chests "Made in China" block the aisles and cheap toy guitars hang from the ceiling.

"You can have the zoo animals, son."

Mam forks over a quid to the blue-coated woman behind the register.

I'm already deep in the jungles of Africa, being stalked by a lion: a lion whose razor-white teeth will tear the flesh on my forearm and accompany me in play and dreams for night after night, as Jesus, bloody heart in hand, looks down from the bedroom wall.

I keep a secret cotton-wooled in a painted box. A floating secret, light as red feathers, heavy as the thump of a dead tree-limb falling on drifted snow. The wish for the death of my Old Man. A building ululation wells from my larynx, the Adam's apple palpates with a steady rhythm. Out the window a silent white seabird stands on one leg, the skinny limb supporting its body's weight; the bird's punkish crest ruffles in the breeze.

I let go of the sound—the kept vowels and consonants of grief. Watch them escape into the air, like a caged creature given an open door. The wail goes out into the world, tears through the air and fills the brimless vessel of the day.

4

—Dreams.

—Of an ancient monument in a garden, a stone flag with a monkey atop.

—I'm imprisoned in my old school, in a large room with windows. Men are working outside. I know I'm going to get out and at some point I remember talking to two people inside the room and discussing who would write the book. Grimy windows, cleaning off the dust, seeing workers outside.

—I was dying, and the last gesture I made was to gather the brown earth with my two hands and grasp it to me. I became a being devoid of facial features, limbs, etc. There was a process of gathering together limbs and attempting to relive life as a shadow person of sorts. I ended up burning down the family compound and running around helping everyone escape.

—I am stuck on a ledge, like a giant kitchen out of doors. There's a huge drop. I'm way above it and can't quite get back to level ground. I start throwing things off the ledge—part of the ledge itself even. I'm still not able to make it off. I have a terrible fear of falling and there are two other people there who don't really help me. At some point I throw something into the air and it hits a big table and a pot spills. I think it's chicken stock. But the pot doesn't overspill because there's a large metal roasting pan (huge) under the table that holds all the liquid. I cling by my fingertips, afraid of falling. I do get down, by half-stumbling, half-falling, without help from two bystanders.

BEDWETTER

Say the moon tumbles through the open curtains of your aunt's house and casts the crooked shadow limbs from the tree outside on the wall. Say the shadow looks like the bent outline of a crone, and say she's the old lady from number twelve who died a week ago. Say the flit of owl's wings on the wall makes it look as if she's going to grab you by the neck. What then? Do you cry out in the dark and waken the house, or do you cringe beneath the tucked sheets and wiggle your toes inside the hot water bottle cover for courage?

You don't want Da to think you're what he calls a "namby pamby gossoon," do you? This is why you suffer the wetness of the bed when you feel the pee coming and you aren't able to get out of the bed and make it to the toilet. Da calls you "piss the bed," and tells Mam you should wash your own bloody bed sheets. You overheard Mam with Mrs. Standish, and how she whispered the words "delicate lad."

This is why you bundle the sheets up in a ball and sleep under the bed. This is why twenty-eight years later your wife will sleep in a separate bedroom. Why she arranges for you to see the hypnotist, and then the acupuncturist, and then the psychic. When she asks why you started wetting the bed after ten years of marriage, you haven't an answer for her.

Say she knew the truth. Say she dragged her acrylic nail from your navel to your Adam's apple and split you in two, letting the old hag out into the thin night air of the house on Pennington Street. What then? What could you possibly do to hide from the ghost living inside your bladder for all these years?

Say she says, "If I'd known you were a bedwetter I'd never have married you."

Say you take your wet pajama pants off and creep into the corner beside the dresser with the picture of your Da and Mam in the silver frame you bought from the small antique store on Regina Street. What are you going to do for the rest of the night as the tree shadows climb the wall and the crone comes out of the wardrobe where she's been biding her time? From twenty-eight years distance, Da's voice mocks you as you huddle naked against the wall.

TELL MY WIFE I'M SORRY

The night before the morning after our marriage sank into the kelp-thick bay. My wheels spin, the sky downside up, the Cooper's hawk whistles derisively, and nothing moves forward. I follow the scaled carapace, snap-off tail, a yellow-green frog leaps into infinity along the fence line. My daily bread, the crushed leaves, the scarred flesh of olive-green avocados—dream of shame. *Ele-mental*—a tribe of grass circles, miniature depressions in the ground, some measure of comfort given, the crepe billows in the trees. She banishes me to the waters and the wild.

"Whose are those scrawled notes on the paper in your office?" she asks.

"Certainly not mine." Spoken like a true renegade. Integration of tooth and tongue, reiteration of blasphemy carried out on the front lawn of a Middle Ages church. The accusation wavers in the distance.

Count the hairs on the back of the hand—the darker ones soon turn an autumnal cadence. If a corner is split by a jagged line does that mean the obtuse becomes the obverse?

When she says I can run as far as possible—into corners where thin-blooded spiders spun webs of dismay—I take no note of her words, instead seventeen varieties of silken webs are collated into a wrist adornment and I contemplate the open road.

At night, lying between the cheap sheets of a crack motel, the dreams unravel, a collection of groans, the pillow soaked with sweat. In the province of regret I make a flailing attempt to staunch the flow of "should have dones" and "if wishes were horses." And when morning comes, the torn confetti of wedding photos floats away on the breeze.

CHILDBIRTH

Ovens, sofas, upside-down strollers—shapes that appear out of the mist on the drive from Baton Rouge to Lafayette. He entered the water, barefoot, stick cradled, knuckles scarred from last night's bar fight, where ordinary men backed away and left the gathering to those who knew better. Careful footfall after careful footfall, he searched for the curved trail of water moccasin in motion. A decent-sized one glided by, tongue y-ing the air, and with a painter's patience he grabbed the snake by the neck, writhing from the water. Hooking one leg around a tree limb, he planted the head against a green Kenmore fridge and brought the stick down on the skull. A deflated sound from the snake and it shrank into the belt it would become. He swung about and waded for shore. At home, his wife sweated in the back bedroom, hours from birthing twins, as the whistle of the evening freight from Houston drew close.

GREEN THEIR DEAD EYES

An oratory crumbled to ruin sits in the shade of the mountain. Once, monks prayed hard into the rain and gathered honey from the thrumming hive. Now, blood-glutted bees skim the furze and enter the ancestral blooms. Away on the mountaintop the dead fester under a clouded morning. Their hearts have stopped, their mouths have ceased to breathe, and a storm approaches over the Atlantic.

Three wooden crosses staked in the ground, the rocky, dry soil of Ben Bulben's plateau. The crucified: an island-man from Achill who'd stolen bread from a window ledge to feed his twelve motherless children, a cooper from Drumlish who "borrowed" a lamb from an isolated field, and a schoolteacher, who refused to say morning prayers. Cold skin, heavy limbs, too large a price for their crimes. The sheen of the distant ocean greened their dead eyes.

Corncrake, curlew, fieldfare—birds of witness, birds of mourning, swing down and around the crossed trio. Rain in sheets blows east across the mountain, the shingles on ramshackle whiskey stills rattle in the nowhere. On the sandy shore tarred hulls face the sky like dead beetles, their ebony surfaces slick from salted water. The witnesses are down off the mountain now, safe and dry at home.

PRIVILEGE

The dreams are always the same. The woman with a gold spoon where her left arm should be, the way her childish smile cracks in two like an egg fallen from the nest. The passage in *Ulysses* about the Andalusian girls lies open on the table, a cup of coffee, untouched. When the daddy longlegs stipples its way down the wall and mouths the spoon it is one of the great wonders of the night. Jessamine scented—the life of the page-bound woman—she is bold scented, a lime fragrance, the simple chain about her thin neck. Her spoon feeds me the cod liver oil capsule, a Monday morning ritual corrupting the nighttime.

ROADKILL

I pound the street and my sacroiliac throbs mightily as the dead skunk roadside pours its scent out for all it's worth and the white fur trembles in the soft breeze and even though I wear my dark cloak of sadness I find something humorous in the silence of the smashed creature the way its body splays like a knockout victim in a boxing match on TV the angle of the limbs unreal the timing couldn't be better as the approach of a speeding F-150 forces me into the side of the road and my heel touches the corpse and the blurred text on the door of the truck goes by and I give the driver the finger me in my sporty outfit him in his overalls and USC hat me suddenly realizing he was probably the one to slay the animal and as I approach the intersection where I'll turn left to head home a couple argues over a minor traffic altercation the girl having a freakout and the guy picking at his chinos bought on sale at Target the plastic security tag filled with ink still attached and I wonder if he stole them or what?

THE HANDSOMEST MAN
IN THE PARISH

The Christian ladies marched to prayer, their blindfolds tight, their delicate necklaces stirring on starched collars. I knelt behind them in the cold stone church, the chink of the censer and the sweetness of the smoke enough to distract the other churchgoers from the captives with their shined shoes and white linen gloves. As the priest swung the chained vessel one last time the ladies bowed their blindfolded heads in deference to the ringing of the bell by the chief altar boy.

It was as if they were mutoscopic images, positioned inside a faded, red metal casing, and the congregation the patient viewers waiting their turn to be amazed. When the prayer began their mouths moved in beautiful lipsticked ovals, rose and cherry and pale pink, the words like released butterflies, floating up to the stained-glass ceiling.

During the sermon the folded gloves sat on laps like pale fish, the buttons, eyes, the stitching, ribs. The priest, a swarthy fellow from Leitrim, took a fit of coughing and had to be taken from the altar to the sacristy for relief by way of water. Behind their blindfolds their eyes followed chains of colorless molecules up and down the insides of closed lids as the parishioners fidgeted and whispered gossip until the priest returned to the pulpit.

Repeating himself, he proceeded to reiterate the church's position on heresiarchs. The blind ladies' heads turned in unison towards their keeper. The doctor adjusted his eyeglasses and stroked his narrow barb of beard, his eyes fixed on hanging Jesus' bloodied side. As the handsomest man in the parish, the Frenchman was admired from a distance by all the wives of the working men. His charm, his opinions of all matters of taste and decorum, his decorative sword that swung from his side, were simply wonderful, they said.

BATTLE

Nothing prepares you for the breaching of the waters, the spout fluming into air, the lusty cry of new life. When the mucus and womb-matter are brushed away and the fierce flush of red blood courses through the body, there's a flood of pure unreasoned joy.

Her name falls from my lips. The tuft of black hair, the bluest of eyes, a memory of my long-dead father: his presence in the operating room, stoic in the corner. It echoes the lines from Anita Diamant's *The Red Tent*:

Why did I not know that birth is the pinnacle where women discover the courage to become mothers? But of course there is no way to tell this or hear it. Until you are the woman on the bricks, you have no idea how death stands in the corner, ready to play his part.

Death waits in the corner for days—folded arms, patiently watching over the struggle—unmoved by the battle for new life. Death is satisfied with what she sees—the pitched battle between effort and exhaustion—and pronounces the struggle acceptable.

And what of our daughter, destroyer of souls, singer from some wine-dark sea? Now, she rests—her stuttering entry into the oxygen world over—and calms with poetry and song. A thin red line connects us, one to the other, the songline of which an old friend speaks.

I was not there when my son entered this same oxygen world, but something gives way inside me and Yeats' words echo in the newly minted chambers of my bigger heart— "All changed, changed utterly. A terrible beauty is born."

Now our songline sings her song from unclogged lungs, her roving eyes searching for her tribe. Together we go out into the oxygen world to stride the wave-thick waters and watch for seals in the surf.

JAM JAR

Yellow stripes. A curtain. Summer dress. Strawberry blonde. Remind me of years ago. Thinner. Prettier. Not much older. Been there, seen that, walked the streets. Nice to put context to abstraction. Young. Not so young. A beach, sand, toes, shine of sun, the hills pretty distant, your skin quite pale.

Fill in the spaces. Once, during high school you were depressed. When your mother lost her mind because her hips were so wide. She ate chocolate fiendishly, even the salty kind you thought she'd leave alone. A dog, you suggested. A husky, or a malamute. Force her to exercise.

In the noontime rush the barista is testy, does a little dance, gets a dollar tip. Over half-way through the book. Requirement. Split down the center. Buttons, or would you prefer half-and-half? Oh, a long time ago I had a crush on a girl just like you. Her mother didn't approve. Catholic Ireland. Parochial. Provincial. All of the above. In truth, I wanted you not to fret, not to worry, nor cry. There's boredom in your eyes, still as standing water. In secret we'd invent sins for the priests to forgive in the confessional. We had an old parish priest, a creep, loved to hand out decades of the Rosary as penance. Little wonder I stopped going to Mass. He had a brindled beard, salt-and-pepper, they call it. Man made me nervous. I never went back.

The Czechs are marvelous. But the South Americans? Have you read them? A world of wonder awaits. Amazing to be on that path, beginning again, the page blank, the linen soft to the touch. By the window we could talk of sins, and dust-covered books, and the open pitcher of honey ale we'd swig from before undressing. You know, the Marxist would be insanely jealous? Yes. He might react in a not-too-pleasant manner. The soft curve of bone where the clavicle dips flashes in front of my eyes and I knock the jam jar of tea to the ground.

PREHISTORY

I wonder how long it took you to get dressed? The line of hooks and eyes on the back of your shirt looks too complicated for one person to manage. Maybe your mother helped you. I remember the cross she left the house with in the mornings at weekends. How she strode in circles under the statue of Parnell, paper rosettes pinned to her coat, the prayers falling like raindrops from her lips. All those years, you never spoke of her crusade against the promiscuous, only ignoring the barbs of those who knew, but were too embarrassed to tease you about her.

Light from outside paints your face a gently washed pink, the down a faint halo about you. The curve of your back reminds me of a rowan tree bending in the wind, the strength of the hard wood. The time you had all four wisdom teeth extracted at once, we sat on the couch, the two dogs sunk in pillows, your cheeks swollen, the H.B. Neapolitan's ice cream's sections melting from the fire's heat. Now, everything is different, the shape of our lives a prolonged trajectory of disappointments. I heard you'd lost a baby at term, the careful months of preparation wasted.

Later, maybe tonight, I shall wear my hat—the one with

the ear-flaps—and listen to some old rock-and-roll, Cream perhaps, or Frampton Comes Alive. Despite the closeness of the street I will sing the words aloud, halfway between the kitchen and the back bedroom. Our dog-walking neighbor with the three Jack Russells might stare in at me, the bells on their collars ringing with impatience. If there's a decent moon she'll make out my handsome face, the notching of an arrow in my bow, the way my feet slide on hardwood floor. More likely, I'll go unnoticed, the same way I've done for most my life.

We can meet in the margins of your book, between Tuesday night and Wednesday afternoon. Will you use the pear-scented soap, the one I bought for you at l'Occitane en Provence? I sat at the same table every day for two weeks and imagined another life. The owner twirled the tips of his mustache between thumb and forefinger as his daughter smoked cigarettes and poured my *café-au-lait*, the southern sun shadowing the territory between skin and lace.

Church bells ring across wet rooftops, a ping-pong of iron on iron. The back garden where we lay in summer and flirted poorly is now a swamp. The snails float on shells, their feelers are paddles, their undercarriages useless. I know I was an idiot to test the waters of love. Those roses I gave you should have been delivered somewhere else, but I wanted what I couldn't have. We can laugh about it now in the time we have left to remember our shared moments. In the distance between peals I count the pleats in your striped sundress and confetti your freckles in the air.

HEADACHE

The soft spot where the plates meet never closed properly when I was a child. I rest ice cubes there and freeze that part of my brain that lurks beneath hair and skin. I am lonely, and have no interest in other people anymore. There was a pretty girl from North Dakota, but she left me for her therapist. All that remain are an empty bank account and a shitty job at the corner diner in Hell's Kitchen, where I flip eggs over easy and grill sausage patties from 5 AM to noon seven days a week.

I got the news about her death the same day the ice cubes shut my eyesight down for a while. Her mother, a German woman from Bad Kreuznach, a small spa town with a sloping bridge across the Nahe River, told me of an aggressive form of breast cancer. I hung up, took the pictures of the two of us from a drawer and sat by the fire cursing disease and God in the same breath. I cried for her loss, punched the wall between the neighbors' and my place, and settled into the thick fog of sadness that started to leak from the light fixtures.

She had a bumpy nose, something I thought was her best feature, but which was in actuality the reason she left me. I was the only man in the world ditched because he loved his girlfriend's crooked nose. That's how she met the therapist. She found him in the phone book and soon enough was seeing him for an hour a week. Thinking of how he must feel now she's dead, I place on top of my head the spoon from the hot tea I just made. The pain bores right through my soft spot all the way down my back to the groin and I scream in agony. Reflexively, I kick over the small table the tea and photographs are on. The images blur and the dead girlfriend fades away.

NYLON FOLDS OF OLDNESS

She layered yellowish foundation on with a brush she found in the melted leftovers of an ice pop at the bus stop. Flies buzzed about the sticky mess. Dust to dust, the priest said, the day they buried her mother. She wore no make-up, only the lace mantilla she discovered at the bottom of mother's handbag. A man, that was what she wanted. To have him feast on her the way the flies consumed her skin. A man with a straight back and a stack of bills in his wallet. She'd dreamt of such a thing. The spot on her chin gave her hell. Too much powder. At the chemist's shop, between the loofahs and the lemon verbena soap, she'd seen one of those zit removers. If she'd only had the money, or if she'd been brave enough to slip it in her pocket while the man was serving the fellow asking about tartar-removing toothpaste. Her stockings were rolling nylon folds of oldness, remainders from her dead mother's wardrobe. She scratched her scalp vigorously and a clump of gray-red hair came away. Who would want her with bald spots on her head?

WE SUNK MY MOTHER'S MOTHER

A patch of bare earth in the back garden by the begonias. The metal frame of the deck chair wore the grass away over the course of the summer we sunk my mother's mother beneath the dark waters of the dammed Poulaphouca waterfall. That was the summer before Elvis died. I'd gotten a Kodak Instamatic for my birthday and didn't know how to use it properly. Fourteen, awkward, skinny-legged, and with a touch of the OCD about me. She interrupted my counting the cracks in the pavement when she arrived in my uncle's old Rover. Crack, crack, crack. *Step on a crack, break your mother's back.* My granny's back was arched, an overburdened stalk, the flower it supported dried now, her eyes twin anthers of a lost cause. By October she was gone, and remained in her bed, cold and uncomplaining for several weeks before we took her back to her people.

Oar by oar, the blade severed ripples, the red-painted prow cutting through lake water. In a blanket wrapped, her bones stiff and the marrow cold, we rolled the blanketed corpse into the deep. In the late-evening sun of a midland's autumn I watched my childhood bubble and break the surface. My father sat on the wet board, the oar-handles resting on his lap, my mother pushing the beads of the Rosary through, thumb over index finger, the Hail Mary hosanna-ing into the warm air. Together, my parents prayed for the repose of Granny's soul, as her wrapped remains sank to the waiting graveyard. On the way back to shore the muffled bells rang out, and the ghosts of Blessington Village made their way to the church.

BIRDCAGE

I was born with a chirp in my heart. At first my parents rarely paid it any attention, but when the beak began pushing against my skin and the sharp outline threatened to puncture me, they summoned the doctor.

He reached into his cavernous satchel and withdrew a small jar of bird food. "Open wide," he said, and pushed a pincer-grip of seed into my mouth. I coughed, teared up, and wailed. The chirping got louder, and the beak staccatoed against my rib, the drumbeat of hunger.

The doctor took my parents aside and whispered something to them. I was too far away to hear, but whatever was spoken must have been bad, because my mother slumped to the floor and cried out loud. After arguing for a few minutes, my father said, "All right. Do what you must."

Hands entered the satchel again, and this time withdrew a small tool. My father held me down as the doctor sawed through the side of my chest cavity and exposed the ribcage. The small bird struggled to escape between two ribs, but was already too big for the opening. The doctor used a wad of cotton wool and Mercurochrome to dry the blood around the hole, and when he finished he drugged me with something that smelled like old socks soaked in petroleum.

When my parents saw the makeshift cage and the bird with its feathers all stuck together with dried blood, the word "unsustainable" was used. The worm my mother held out was snatched from her fingers and swallowed in a flash. "Maybe there's a book we could read," she said. The doctor shook his head and said, "No book. This is a completely new field." He packed the satchel, crammed the saw into a side-pocket, and tipped his hat to my parents.

The bird was freaking out, flapping its wings, croaking noises escaping from its mouth. "Spend some time with it," he said, pulling the door shut behind him. My mother said, "Let me see you to the door," leaving me alone with my father and the small creature loose in my chest.

The sun filtered in the window, my father's shadow on the wallpaper, the artistic swirls and flourishes traveling floor to ceiling. He clucked at the bird, clicked his fingers, made flapping motions with his arms, but the bird sat on top of my heart, silent. "It's a dead loss," my father said. "You've a real botch job to contend with now." He sat on the end of the bed, rested his chin on his hands and watched several gray seagulls pass across the rooftops.

BED-MAKING

Owls in flight leave no fingerprints on their murder weapons. The joke told, the fire stoked, the child still awake and begging for another bedtime story, not enough energy in this world to begin anew. It's pitch outside, the old tree groans in the wind, roots straining against gravity and the inevitable.

I had a twin once, a fire-haired sister who knew my thoughts before they formed on my lips as crude expressions of desire. She died on the edge of reason, her heart split in two where the pinprick was found. When Mam beat the tiny coffin with her fists the hollow bangs failed to rouse my sister. The brass plate had only her name and the three years of her short life inscribed in florid script.

The hospital said there was nothing they could have done. The lawyer with the office beside the butcher's shop disagreed. Mam said he smelled of raw meat and was not to be trusted. She made my sister's bed the day after the funeral, and the day after that, and for every other day. The house became Mam's prison, her life-sentence.

I stroll across the road to the dairy store to buy her cigarettes. Red-faced white-coated man offers me a light if

I want to smoke, too. Fingers like Denny's sausages, eyes to match, his smile floats in a face of nothingness. Mam and I spoon Knorr Florida Vegetable soup down, toast fingers with butter, and hot cups of tea. The radio hisses and kicks to the weather forecast. Stormy at first, scattered showers with winds from the Northeast. The call of a great horned owl ripples across the field as I attach the hood to my anorak and walk the mile to sister's grave.

SPOON-FED SALIVA

My old math teacher loved Aquinas and quoted him paraphrasing St. Paul over and over: "When I was a child, I spake as a child, I understood as a child, I thought as a child: but when I became a man, I put away childish things." I paid him no attention, preferring to draw in my copybook and reimagine the wonders of the ancient world. Bold as brass, my mother said I was, the Monday I arrived home from school with hands raw from the bamboo cane. I was sent to bed without supper and that spelled the arrival of the dream.

In the nightmare, I was shot in the liver. The woman who pulled the trigger was eight-foot tall, gold-skinned, and earrings made from playing card guitar picks dangled from her lobes. Shrieks interrupted my sleep, and when I sat up in bed everything was covered in a bright green liquid. The woman cradled me by the back of the neck, blood welling beneath, and spoon-fed me her saliva.

"You must stop telling lies," she said, her voice low and raspy. "Didn't your parents teach you anything at all?"

Into green, blue, red, everything blended bold-hued against once-white sheets. Maybe it was a dream, I thought, but when I took a finger away from my side it was damp and sticky. If I managed to survive to morning, I swore to list all my sins, that chain of errors that stretched all the way back to childhood. She didn't listen, only closed her two enormous hands over my mouth and pressed down forever.

BELOVED GO WITH GOD

Flakes of snow tumbled from thick sky onto the uneven pavement as he made the pilgrimage to the burial ground. Greasy bangs fell in front of his eyes, the hair touching his eyeglasses, the sucking of the slush underfoot marking the rhythm of his morning's progress. At the intersection, stripped trees pointed skyward, branches clodded with snow, the steady drop of melt-water creating a narrow river from the cemetery to the road.

He hiked up his corduroy pants over the dirty cotton socks and exposed thin, twig-like legs covered with wisps of dark, curling hair. The remains of morning grits stained his three-day beard, and gloved fingers touched his chin seven times in circular motion before he mounted the few stone steps leading to the graves. The directions were correct, and a collection of objects were laid out on the gravestone: a tin of chew, an almost-empty bottle of Jack Daniel's, Laphroaig Scotch, several dull pennies, and a tattered paperback.

Not wanting to disturb the dead, he leaned against a tree trunk a ways from the headstone, stuck the gloves in his back pocket and with skill rolled a cigarette, pushing the flakes of tobacco into the tube with a fingertip. He puffed away, the pleasure of the hot smoke warming him some. Maybe later he'd find his way to the hardware store and buy those brass hinges the back screen door needed.

He had bluffed his way into the house, the widow polite as could be, offered him iced tea and triangle-cut sandwiches. An old school friend, he'd said. Even though she didn't recognize his name, she asked him to stay a while. On the flagstones he read the names. Simple carving, nothing of note. BELOVED GO WITH GOD. A bubble of grief burst on cracked lips.

THE RIBBONED CORPSE COLD

When I was six there was a hollow recess in my chest where the parasite lived. Mam warned us about the dangers of getting a "worm." She meant a tapeworm, brought about from dirty hands, or undercooked meat. Dinners were burnt offerings, the blackened flesh of fowl and beast, duck with more crunch than autumn leaves, chains of Denny's sausages like iron. She bought the cheap cuts, the fatty bits—poor people's food. If we dared protest, the wooden spoon would be raised above Mam's head.

The worm grew, fed on grains of rice and remnants of pear-flavored Heinz baby food. My secretive friend ribboned and formed into a small mound of pasta-like material. I tickled him under his non-head, the worm-eyes plaintively searching for more food. My friend crept from under my sweatshirt and surrounded a gleaming pile of yeast. The bit on my finger tasted awful, and I ate a stale crust instead and waited for him to finish. In the morning, the worm was still, the ribboned corpse cold against my skin. Mam went across the road for a cup of tea with our neighbor, and I buried the tapeworm in the flower bed, under her favorite hydrangea.

WORK WEEK

The finch in the cage let out a chirp when I skinned my knuckle on the doorjamb. It was the foul state of its tiny space that caused me to masquerade as a shadow boxer and slam my fist against the wood. The bearing of responsibility was proving a little more than I could manage in the aftermath of the shuttering of the toy factory. Willingness to work wasn't an issue in my case.

I had her spoon the lukewarm broth into my mouth. Not only was using a spoon challenging, but the act of handwriting, the only solace left to me, was beyond my wounded abilities. I spent the evening staring at sparks from the wood fire in the grate, contemplating how to extricate myself from the mess I'd managed to make of my post-factory life.

The piazza was a long way back in the corridor of my memory, happier days and nights, traveling by train across Europe, the weathered stone churches passing us at dead of night. Now she put butter on my bruised knuckles and told me she didn't care about the travel. All she wanted, she said, was for the butter to soften so she could make cookies for our tea.

That she didn't console me was what mattered. All we

had was this mediocre life, my job at the toy factory, her work as a sorter of jumble at the abandoned children thrift shop, and our love. Nice of her not to pry about why I'd been laid off. Greater restraint than I'd ever be able to show. She did leave the classifieds on my chair each morning as a reminder.

BOLT THE DOOR

The curtains are always shut in my grandmother's bedroom, the air camphor-thick. She kneads the rosary beads and mutters "Hail Holy Queens" and "Our Fathers," and never ventures outside, save to be driven to Sunday Mass by Da. She looks like one of those old women in the Grimm Brothers' stories, ready to lure me into her lair.

One day, Mam knocks on the bedroom door and comes into our room. *Your grandmother is dead,* she tells me. *Say a prayer for her with me.* We kneel by the bed, Mam and me. *For the repose of her soul,* Mam says. *Hail Mary, full of grace…*

Da drives us all down the country to Granny's funeral in Athlone. I've never seen a corpse before. In the parlor of my uncle's house before the undertakers take the coffin to the church, she lies, dried out—the rosary beads entwined in her right fist and the picture of Saint Thérèse of Lisieux in the other.

In Coosan cemetery, the coffin rests on two planks of wood as fists drop clay onto the shiny lid. By a chain link fence several old women shuffle toward the grave, rosary beads clutched in their hands. Ravens pick at the side of the road in solidarity.

After her death I begin to see and hear her ghost. It's at night she scares me the most. The mumbled groans from behind her bedroom door. Granny, lying there, rigid, arms by her sides, her watery eyes fixed on the ceiling. The luminous hands of the alarm clock point to 3 a.m. and I swear I can smell her rose water perfume, and hear the dry bones cracking in the next room. This is stupid because she's dead, and I saw them put her in the grave. The floorboards creak on the landing and I pull the sheets up to my chin. Another creak and I slide under the coverlet.

I emerge from my hiding place an hour later. Only my father's snores can be heard. I creep out of bed and search for my slippers in the dark. I shuffle to the door and put an ear to the wood. Nothing. I can't open it. My bladder strains. I need to pee. She might be out there on the landing. I can't do it. Instead, I open my cotton pants and let the yellowish pee leak onto the wallpaper. I shake my mickey and creep back to bed and cry into the pillow.

That's the beginning. The nightmares. In some of them she beckons me from her deathbed. The picture of Jesus. His staring, mournful eyes. The beating heart. Bloodstained walls. I wake, saturated with sweat.

Afterwards, lying in bed with the hot-water bottle cold at my feet, the weak odor of wetted leaves wafts under the door, the bathroom too far away from the safety of the bedroom.

Night after night I recreate this shameful ritual. In the mornings I try to forget everything. Instead of skulking in the dark and dribbling pee down the wall, I know I have to face my fears. So, one night, I open the door, inch-by-inch, and sprint along the landing, stumble down the three steps to the toilet, the presence of *something* behind me. I pull the bathroom door shut and slide the deadbolt across to save my life. I'm comforted by the sound of my pee trickling into the water. Breathing heavily, I pull the door open and run back up the stairs to my bed and fall into a deeper sleep.

A few weeks later, walking home from school, I stand on the same spot we found Granny that one day she disappeared from our house in her nightgown. The house is a big, abandoned Edwardian, next-door to Lahart's Garage. A force draws me toward the house, the corrugated iron over the front door filled with graffiti and torn posters advertising Fossett's Circus and Christmas pantomimes of years gone by. I hoist my schoolbag higher and enter the overgrown front garden, the air full of the smell of spilled motor oil and rubber tires.

Long shadows from the horse-chestnut tree in the front yard trail up the red-bricked walls. Virginia creeper crawls everywhere, all the way up to the eaves where a sparrow bobs in and out of a wood-knot, almost hidden by the ivy.

At the side of the abandoned house lay broken ladders and ancient paint buckets covered in dribbles, the same blue-royal as the eaves. The smell of the paint is omnipresent. I hug the wall as if at any moment the entire house will consume me. Beads of sweat collect on my forehead. A tight fist squeezes my walnut-sized heart.

Swallowing hard, my chest still hurts. Inside, a giant hole in the floor exposes the basement twenty feet below. A few planks of flooring and ceiling fragments jut out from the walls. In the web-strewn corner of the room, elevated four feet above the broken floorboards, my grandmother floats, her white hair shines and her crooked finger beckons. Something gives way and my pants dampen. I sprint home, run up the stairs, into the toilet, bolt the door, slump to the floor, and sob.

LIVER SPOTS

As a yellowish mud pools about the piano, a thick swarm of flies swims, intent on smothering all life out of the air. The buzzing of the broken air-conditioner gives to the day a dreamlike sense. Someone has drawn a smiley face in the dust that covers the piano stool, ignoring for one moment the stack of sheet music that spills to the ground.

She's a fragment of who she was before the operation. Daddy, of all men, says, "Of course it matters," and how her hair comes out in clumps; the chemo strips her down to essentials. In the chair with the straight back he picks at the liver spots on the backs of his hands, the evening air rolling through the house with the queasy certainty of a coming storm. Her ballet-slippered foot pumps the pedal and the notes stack up on top of each other, towering, flailing, falling minuets.

FRAGMENTS OF THE BIRD

OPEN WINDOW

The day the Bird died, Mairé was hanging wet laundry on the washing line in the far meadow. A soft wind billowed the bed sheets, and grayed, lace bloomers swayed romantically, having seen better days. Olivia, her neighbor from across the road, made her way down the narrow path, waving her hands in the air, making sure to avoid the nettles on either side.

"The Bird is dead, isn't he," Mairé said.

"How did you know?" Olivia said, pulling the collar of her coat tight.

"Didn't a crow fly into the upstairs bedroom last night at dusk." She spoke through a mouthful of clothespins, the words splintered, her tightly curled hair not moving in the breeze.

FLUSTERED

He was the first man to touch her that way. His breath beery, his hands warm, the show-band playing a slow song, the bandleader combing his brilliantine hair with a plastic comb, lisping the words onto the dance-hall air. Later, in the back of the Bird's '38 Ford he slipped his two ferret hands up her skirt and took what he wanted. The next month she married the bugger who owned the bar and the Bird drank down the road at Hourican's for a long while. When he finally returned to his familiar seat he could see the swell of her belly under the apron. A lucky man, the bar owner, the Bird thought, regretting his inaction at the wedding mass and how when the priest had asked if any man present...

BANTAM

Three colorful bantam hens pecked in the dirt in the narrow space behind the public house. One had the bright, sharp eyes of a born killer. The Bird weighed the coins in his pocket, doing the math as to how much it would cost to purchase the creature.

"I'll give you two sovereigns for the bantam with the bright eyes," he said to the man behind the bar.

"I can't sell you the bantam. It's the lad's pet. His mother would have my guts if I sold the child's pet for fighting."

"Are you going to let a woman tell you what you can or cannot do in your own house?" the Bird said, his left eyebrow raised.

"It's easy to see you're a bachelor. If you had a wife of your own you'd be singing a different tune."

The Bird grunted, tipped the glass and emptied the porter in one go. "You're a foolish man to turn down two sovereigns," he said, touching the brim of his hat and heading for the door.

NAMES

The doctor placed the tiny baby in its mother's arms. Sure, it didn't weigh more than a bag of flour, as fragile and ugly as a newborn bird.

When the bar owner saw the little mite in his wife's arms, the sharp beak of a nose, the dark eyes, the curl of matted hair, he recognized a family likeness not his own.

"He's like a wee bird," he told her.

"Yes, but he's our little bird," the mother said, squeezing her husband's hand.

He was not so sure. Not so sure at all.

NIGHTTIME

The bantams went wild when the creature slipped in the shed door. Feathers and shit flew everywhere, and the fox, if it were a fox, grabbed one by the neck and blooded it out. All that remained of the three birds was the pile of feathers on the ground, the blood splattered all over the floor. A desperate thing, the Bird agreed with the bar owner as he told him about the brazen fox that had savaged the child's pets. The Bird fingered his winnings and thought about buying the man's lad a rabbit instead.

SWEET SHOP

In the line at the shop the lad held his mother's hand and rubbed the back of his leg with the toe of his shoe. From behind, the Bird recognized the shape of the earlobes and his heart tightened.

"How's the Bird?" Mrs. Flavin asked from the counter.

He reddened, coughed, muttered, "Game ball, game ball."

The mother turned around and gave him a look that spoke volumes in its silence.

"How's the lad, Mairé?" he asked.

She put the *Woman's Weekly* and the boy's lucky bag on the counter and banged down her coins.

VALVIC

AORTA

The heart is an engine, an engine, an engine. Four chambers thump away, an enigma, an enigma, an enigma. We are on the beach late one night, the tide full in, the shush of wave and wash full-echoing in the dark, her scarred, pitted face bright against a backdrop of cloud. In the syzygy of incoming water she is on her back, the moon in her eyes, panting, heavy-bodied, my mouth on hers, the bitter taste of coffee, fatal jabs to the heart.

The rock is a bed, the sky a cabin, the moon a lamp, and she is all I can handle and more, now one of the chambers of my heart has ceased to beat, closed its valvic opening, failed in its task. I feel sleepy, the rush of blood in my inner ear resonates with the to-and-fro of the ocean, and her body is laid out on the rock like laundry sinking into the porous sandstone, the rail of her tongue weakened, the shine of her eyes a memory.

SAPIUM

The scut, a young lad of no more than fifteen, sees me pouring sugar into the petrol tank. One of the *intifada*, he leaves me on the flat of my back, the bullet lodged in the base of my skull, the exact spot where last summer a tick embedded and gorged on my blood. For weeks the skin cracked, flesh exposed, its torsoless legs tunneled into the skin. The area around the tick hardened, crusted with yellow pus. Fingers found tweezers found tiny legs found purchase and withdrew them one at a time. The swollen area is a crater on a distant planet now, the fuzzy image beamed back to earth from months away.

I am flying forward against a table by the pace of the shot, the collapse to bare floor a sinking into darkness—a signal. Even in unconsciousness the smoke spirals from the barrel, an exhausted trail of witness. I am not dead, only stunned, the duck egg on my forehead caused by impact with a wall. Where the snub-nosed projectile struck is bare of hair since the tick incident. Perhaps it's the shock, maybe something else, but I blurt my pants, and the warmth spreads across my buttocks.

VENA CAVA

The broken valves hiss and sputter; a tightness in my chest from where the wires go in. Every day I swallow a cocktail of pills—blue, red, gray, white, small, oval, large, circular— and drain the tube that leads into the plastic bucket by my bed. I am spun thin, the numbers greening their way across the gray. Tongue thick, throat narrowed to a hair's breadth, my fingers peel and crack; the tissue papery and forlorn.

The dizzying sun behind the muslin curtain, a mirage of all the suns that came before, the orbit elliptical, the stutter-stop-start a queer progression in the morning air. Once I lived across from a lane where we played French cricket with a tennis racket and pitched a threadbare ball through summer air. Now, the air is autumn, the systems shut down, the last innings begun. The wind brings red hair and lost memories.

AUTUMN TINGED WITH MUD

Thaw, puddles softening at the edges, still a silence in the frozen center, a trapped blackberry from autumn tinged with mud. My dream glows about the edges with the pale pink of malice. Sometimes I wish I had been switched at birth, given instead to the traveler in the next bed, sure of a life on the roads in their brightly colored caravan. We were taught to fear strangers, never to accept sweets from them, nor to get into a car with them. A man, the crooked one with the chapped lips, he offered me money—green pound notes, and ten shillings in coins. A snuggle, that's what he said he wanted. Since his daughter had drowned in the Shannon, he used sleep in her room, the teddy bears and dolls arranged neatly on her bed. I had a stuffed zebra, glass eyes, black as the bits of slack on the ground outside our garden shed. It helped keep the nightmares away, the ladies with sharp teeth and violent lipstick, the ones we saw at Mass on Sundays. These ladies are charming, their shiny brooches and perfumed overcoats, prayers falling from their lips like kisses from unwelcome relatives at Christmas.

HER FATHER, A TOMBSTONE

From Prisoner's Harbor you can see all the way to the state beach if you've a mind. The hand covers the mouth, the missing teeth lost somewhere on the strand, his grin, a broken fence of abandoned hopes. The last thing at night, before bats skim the treetops, before owls snatch the old cats from the footpaths, the child smiles at her mother and says, "I believe in fairies."

Interwoven with snapped branches, a gauzy scarf and jet-black wig. The body is sticking up in the sand, crabs gaining purchase on loose skin, the sunlight a disconnected fantasy. He practices a deep faith—a muteness born of infant terror. On the mainland, his daughter is deep in bedtime stories of Peter Pan and Tinkerbell: her safety, uncertain; her father, a tombstone. Eyes of the night are hooked on the promises of tomorrow, when he will come home.

CARAPACE

I came of age in a hollowed-out log, my carapace grown hard, the shimmer of green scoring my underbelly. At the time I wasn't unduly worried by the thought I'd become some self-created godhead. Warmth flowed from the early sun, the dew smoking into air, the influence of a thousand spores lingering in the moment. On the water I saw mallards float by, their smug faces implacable, the impossibility of their capsizing.

Before I arrived at this place I discovered my mother's revulsion, made flesh in the cardboard coffin she shut me in. This life a bed of nails, a discordant and unsettling thing, like some monster hiding beneath the bed. Through a narrow slit I saw her crouch near me, a tear or two in her eye. She made no vow to have and to hold me.

Whatever happened when the spark of my beginning lit, I forgot. Funny how our bodies comply with the rules of nature, goats know to bleat rather than bellow, an unwritten code of being.

THE WATCHER

A teacher self-immolates on a playground somewhere in France, at the same time a farmer in coastal California drives by a dead Cooper's hawk, and says to himself, "Well, I'll come back for the hawk later. I can hang it in the fruit trees to keep other animals away." The weight of an avocado is too much to bear, and the smooth green-skinned fruit thumps to the ground, next to the rotting hawk's corpse.

As the evening church bells ring out over the small French *ville*, citizens line up and place candles and flowers by the statue of the Virgin Mary at the school entrance. Helene, a precocious six-year-old, asks her mother if her teacher will go to heaven. In a nearby tree, a raven tears at the soft, furred chest of a still-alive mouse.

Waves rise and fall on the beach of the Californian town, and a seal blinks hesitatingly in the swell beyond the surfers perched on their egg-shaped boards. Seven brown pelicans glide along behind the surfers, eyes downcast, searching for a glimmer of fish to feed upon. An approaching train whistles with pulmonary steadiness, warning track-crossers of its proximity.

The girl's mother places a burgundy silk scarf over the bedside lamp, casting a dim glow over the room, as a chain of paper birds flocks over the sleeping child. The mother brushes a strand of hair from the child's forehead, and kisses her lightly. Something about the glow of the room in scarf-lit light reminds her of the water in the bath when she birthed her darling.

Later the same day, small birds veer away from the trees, disturbed by the watcher in the high branches.

RETURN TO A WATERY LIFE

Remember that day you caught the sun? When you crested the first of the waves my heart fell as the sleek seal's head disappeared under the swell and did not return. On land I had no idea of the secret harbored inside you, the birthright of Neptune, Poseidon, fish-gods both.

Slope of sun across streaked red sky, the trajectory traced in letters too large for the eye to comprehend. The time you stared through the pinhole at the sun, seared a memory to take beneath the water. Lighthouses cast steady beams, wide and near, the rocks beneath were where we met. Somehow the pelt didn't suit you, and that desire to land on shore became too much.

Crushed sand dollars decorated your hair the first time we danced at the foot of the lighthouse all those years ago. Turn and turn again, the quitting sun splashing fire across the sky, we moved in anti-clockwise circles, the land, the sea, the land again. Every now and then the sun would catch the shimmer of trapped quartz in your hair, blinding flash, terrifying premonition of a return to a watery life. On the edge of the rocks they collected in pairs, saltskinned and apart, no bitter irony in their eyes.

STILL LIFE

Down there, the filthy blankets and beer bottles, 40-oz for cider drinkers, liver problems, cirrhosis, the smell of frying bacon, birdsong, even though they're only pigeons. To die, to die, to die I go, the cobblestone road shining like fish scales in the sun. In school they made me learn the words to "The Lake Isle of Innisfree." Singsong, merry-go-round. Yeats liked the young girls, he did: *pince-nez*, peeper, one-eyed giant. Rusting cans of Bachelor's beans, there's your two brave men, now. Monkey suits and monocles, dapper feckers. She over there used know the inner workings of fifteen hundred file cabinets, government ministry, high heel shoes, severe hairstyle. Never know it to look at her now, pink shiny leggings, torn Ugg boots, Guess American flag t-shirt. The inside of her thighs looks like a crudely plucked Christmas turkey, the hole from the barbs wide and oozing. Life and life and O say can you see by the dawn's early light, before she arrived home with a mother in the John of Gods, paralytic. The apple doesn't fall far. A nod is as good as a wink to a blind man.

Caught looking at day-old pastries in a trash can behind the coffee house, away with the faeries since the fall from the ladder, paint can, yellow walls, the powdered sugar snow in the sunlight. Hands shaking, week-old underwear sticking to cold skin, oh first communion, and the host in my hands, body of... sticking to roof of my mouth, fingers interwoven, holy, holy, holy Lord, God of Hosts. Silence in court, muteness, the house taken away. And the loose change in torn pocket, collected in a rusted can, missing teeth, the way the space holds a hunk of pastry prisoner. House sparrows on the eaves, triangular beaks, like the old Pyramid orange drink from school. Fingers hooked in pants, grin on face, sing a few bars of "Biddy Mulligan, the Pride of the Coombe," before lapsing into fantasy and watching mother spread the table for tea. Go on, move along, now. Does she believe in God that one? Not a Christian bone in her body. Husband mustn't tickle her apostrophe much. Reach in now. Deep is where the good stuff is hidden.

In the Shelbourne Hotel the diners used need jacket and tie to slurp from the trough. Saw the news today, four dead in train derailment. Soft skulls, must have been a bumpy ride, neighbors' luggage flying from overhead bins, and the time my own mother packed a suitcase and threatened to leave. "Alive! Alive-Oh!" The top drawer empty, Mother's pretty things gone, and only on the therapist's couch did the door shut and she came back in to apologize for frightening the wits out of me. In a fog, surrounded by haze, a lonely place for me and my thoughts. Might be able to bore my little finger into the crab-leg and get the meat out. You have a disease, she said, and smiled at me with those eyes. Worked hard, plenty of back pay when I left. Had a cake for goodbye, they did. Hair like fire, her best feature, and I want it back, but what's under the newspapers there? The old fellow used kick the dog at night, quiet him down, he'd say. maybe I'll go back to the shelter, take a bed for a few nights. Three stone faces on top of the bank building. Gaping mouths, manes too. Kick the habit, straight-and-narrow.

Spoiled bananas, browner the better to ward off the big C. That chap over there has a face that'd curdle cream. Look at the pale cheeks on him, a real delicate flower. What if I walked over and laughed in his face? Hazard a guess that he's an accountant. Or an actuary. The color of that tie. Puce. The mother would say the shop assistant saw he came down in the last shower. A good laugh they must have when they sell the unsellable things to the naive. Do they feel guilty? Drops of rain fall, pock-pock-pock the plastic containers. Up umbrellas, pierce the clouds. Might freeze tonight. Sleep under Crossguns Bridge. No bugs in the rotted mattress. Too cold. Ignore me when I try to buy a newspaper. Still like the crossword. Body of Christ, last refuge of sinners. Lost my watch in the shelter. Some shitehawk stole it. Light-fingered. Better off outdoors. Closer to nature. Closer to God. Closer to death.

JAUNDICE

The left is broken. The bones shift in a discomforting way. My crooked nature, the limbic state: devious. Try self-hypnosis, she said. Take some time, consider my request. The natural thing to do is to lace your hands comfortably behind your head, ask the question you have on your mind.

The discovery of a secret is a spectacular moment for the dreamer, and when the urge to sleep comes on you, let it bring you along. I promise, you'll find the answers in the lyric strata of dreams. Finding the moment, the precisely chosen time to flee consciousness, to curl up under the blanket, is so much part of the next steps for you.

My mouth hurt, the ice water griking into explosions of pain. A lifelong fear of dental work—the ginger plant in the office when I took the tour—my resistant shuffle, not at all sure of myself. When I wrote in my diary later that day, it was with my favorite cat, Pig, a jaundice-colored beast, on my lap.

In dreams the math worked out, the minutes to take me to the edge of sleep, the plea with the characters to do their bidden duty, but she was wrong—the idea never came. Instead, the bench at the river is where I go, without writing, interested more in legs and feet, than resolution.

SINGING A BREATHLESS TUNE

Copper kettle, singing a breathless tune on the hob, a switch of willow wand lies by the door, and outside she waits in the shadow of the gable-end of the cottage. When the moths flit by at dusk, dropping intricacies of sand onto her shoulders, there's a warm sensation that comes over her, nameless, without shape, or form. Five words float out of her mouth onto the balmy air, but the moths cannot hear.

By the range, a marmalade cat licks the blood of a battered rat off its claws, blinks its eyes a few times, recalls the rat's struggle to get away. Futile is the cat's name, and futile were the rat's efforts. Clotted cream dries on the counter where the woman spilt the jug earlier, filling scones. The weight of the rat in the belly of the marmalade cat suggests a level of satisfaction that stops the beast from climbing to the sink and licking the cream up.

Outside, a barn owl screeches, a discordant sound. The cat shivers, remembering the feel of owl claws embedded in its head only the previous month.

BACKWARD ACCELERATION

The pieces are lined up on the makeshift board, vying with scraps of tissue, singleton pubic hairs, and flakes of mud from the workman's boots. I like to tell myself better days are ahead, days when I can afford to upgrade to a smartphone and play against a computer. Nothing could be further from the truth. The days pass by in a swirling, backward acceleration, the way I used turn the records backwards on the turntable and hear the Devil's voice urge me to action.

Elvis told me to burn the record shop to the ground. I was playing "The Girl of My Best Friend," for the thousandth time, when the voice groaned to me, "Buuuuuurrrrrrnnnnnn iiiittttt! Uhhhhh hhhhhuuuuuhhh."

The old lady who owned the shop received a check from the insurance company and moved to Fairhope, AL, to live her days out in the Grand Hotel, surrounded by fine art and fine bone china tea service.

"An electric fire," the assessor said. I read it in the weekly newspaper, next to the "pitchforks and halos" section. Someone gave a pitchfork to the local liquor store because of the bundled-up American flag on their roof.

I confess.

Mea culpa.

It was I, said the sparrow, *with my little bow and arrow.*

I am the culprit.

Not a wild child, by any means, not one of the local hooligans, as my mother called my friends. I was a good boy, a model student, polite and kind to all. Why did I do it? you ask. I confess, I do not know rightfully, save to say, the disembodied voice of the King of Rock 'n Roll moved me in a most peculiar way.

Now, I spend my time inspecting local businesses for fire extinguisher compliance, and in the spare minutes when I'm not thinking of the fire I set under the newspaper stack, I play chess against Elvis in the ADA-compliant stall. He prefers it when I listen to Dire Straits' "Sultans of Swing," or Peter Sarstedt's "Where Do You Go to My Lovely," but every so often he gives in and his soft Mississippi voice drawls, "The Girl of My Best Friend" the right way.

HURRIED DEPARTURE

I didn't see the clock, covered as it was in lipstick, smeared there by an angry paramour intent on getting her message across in mauve. It must have been five-ish, or thereabouts. How I knew the time was more to do with the glow across the tops of the trees—that particular pool of yellow that comes in the gloaming around here—than any temporal credit given to my innate mental sharpness.

Anyway, my fault, the crusted desires of the middle-aged man, seeking solace in the pages of the pet lover's magazine. When I saw the recipe for the "gumbo" of goat afterbirth with a tone of jasmine, I couldn't resist. My lady friend arrived for dinner, the room aglow in dim purplish lights from the chiffon scarves placed over the lamps, more an effort to conceal the cracked paint and cobwebbed corners than any romantic notion. Don't misunderstand me, I wasn't looking to roll on the sofa with her, no. She was too proper for such activities, but I did sense benevolence on her part towards me.

The wax rolled down the lit candle, like, well, you know... She accepted a splash of Pinot Noir, from Oregon, and walked through to the kitchen, where the caprine gumbo was bubbling away. In the tangle of bloody afterbirth, a small creature was paddling in the cast iron pot, a perfectly formed three-inch tall goat-child.

My lady friend excused herself to the bathroom, and as the kitchen light struck the stove I flicked at a dust mote floating in the light beam. She did not return to the kitchen, only the slam of the door attesting to her hurried departure.

BARK OF COYOTE

Ants everywhere. Cinnamon-bombed house. Crying owls and trapped crickets. Bark of coyote at night, the protruding cage of ribs a disaster to behold. Nothing gives, no leeway, only the barometric pressure gauge ticking a beat upward, toward stormy. A rotten tooth, or a dead rat? Stink of decay. Three is the loneliest number. All quiet on the flower's surface, the stippled center hiding the crawling insect. Small lives, smaller matter, tickled pink by self-importance, the impudence of being earnest, and the cochlear implant allowed the ancient seafarer to know the difference between the song of innocence and that of despair. Rippled and barbaric, the summer drained away, as lit fires sputtered and tent poles separated. Into thin air, the step off as easy as tying an opened shoelace.

THE NIGHT THE LIGHTS WENT OUT

We sat in the collapsed basement; rain dripped off the snapped beams, wind flapped the rent curtains, and the smell of warm meat rose from the frozen mound in the corner. Four days since the lights went out, five days since the sun had lost its brightness and faded to something akin to a light bulb covered by a towel.

"It smells like turkey," she said, rubbing her one good eye.

"No. I think it's more like mutton," I replied, tugging the lapels tight.

The steam rose from the corpse in ripples, the matted fur stiff, stuck together in places. Where the beast came from we had no idea. Schoolbooks told of them when I was a boy, and cave paintings bore their images in central France. But here, in the dimming days before the lights went out for ever, the thousands-of-years-old flesh softened from the burning embers and the aroma of ancient meat filled our empty bellies.

"Is it safe to eat?" she asked.

"Does it matter?" I asked, running a finger along a tusk, feeling the ridges of ancient battles and noting the dried blood caked in its ridges.

"Not if we're going to die anyway. We can at least feast before it happens." Her eye was wet from the rain, or from crying, and all I wanted to do was huddle up against her and tear the flesh with my crooked teeth.

"I miss the daylight. Don't you want to see the clouds blow across the sky again?" she asked.

"No. I wouldn't care if I never saw the clouds ever again. There's a place by the sea where I'd rather be, where the seals roll in oil-thick water and bark sharply as they play. That's what I want to see again," I said.

She scooted across the bare floor to my side and took both my hands in hers. "What about our daughter? What about her, and the plans we had for her?"

I brushed her bad eye with my lips and hushed her the way a mother hushes a crying child. "She's no concern of ours now. Wherever she was when the sun died is where she'll stay."

Maybe she was in her boyfriend's house by the slipway, or on a plane to somewhere exotic for their anniversary. She was excited for their second year together, I knew that. I rubbed my stubbled chin and felt the dead creature to see if the flesh was ready for eating.

As I tapped the chisel on its bare flank the room shook, as if the ground were going to burst apart. Dust and rubble showered from the jagged hole in the ceiling and more steam left the body as I sat back on my haunches.

"Is this it?" she asked. "Is the world going to end today?"

Whilst I searched for answers to those questions, the tusks shifted, the great fuselage of rib cage expanded, dust billowing from fur, and a roar burst from the creature's shredded trunk. Yes, I thought, this is the end of the world, the coming again of past to present, the unbinding of nature in front of our now damaged eyes.

DEMON

Strewn leaves over cold water, I am in green trunks, the banana spiders inches from my face. The leaves are bruises, camouflage for my body which will soon rest amongst them. Ignoring the freezing east wind, the sun shattering into pieces off the face of my watch, I move out along the thick branch that stretches to the middle of the pond. So strongly it blows, the blood in my cheeks turns away from its force, and a shower of rain falls on the earth.

You have to face your demons, she told me. *You can't keep running away forever.*

Not true, I said.

Instead, I laughed at her, guilty of rejecting her love, thrown off by the narrowness of her wrists, the nothingness of her frame. Dandelion stalks, browned to husks, juniper bugs turned to tiny vessels, the natural decay spread beneath me in all its intricate beauty. Nothing about decay is haphazard—not the veined wings of the dead bluebottles on the window ledge at home, nor the piping call of the warbler above me in the tree—nature's ordered world. Toes grip rough bark, one foot placed deliberately in front of the other, the same slow meditation I practiced on the *Via Crucis* on pueblo land all those years ago. She accused me of flight, of always running away from my responsibilities.

Fight or flight, she said, *fight or flight*.

And on the limb, high over hidden water, my limbs refuse to work and I cannot alight.

BINGO NIGHT

Laundry detergent, bread, cauliflower, nasal spray, deodorant, chili pepper flakes, condoms, half-a-dozen size AAA eggs, crème fraiche, 60-watt light bulbs, *People Magazine*, a DVD of *The Quick and the Dead*, and a shower hat. Linda totes her basket on one arm, the mobile phone cradled against her ear, whilst the other hand scratches beneath the underwire of her brassiere. Her skin is broken, veined and blue, and she itches like fucking crazy.

Tonight she visits her brother-in-law, while her sister, Mavis, goes to bingo in the Parish Hall. Linda can't understand why her sister bothers to go to bingo. Mavis once confided, "the thought of shouting 'BINGO' in front of everyone makes me sick to my stomach." Yet for fourteen years she's played the game every Wednesday night, and for every one of those fourteen years of Wednesday nights, Linda has secretly been fucking her sister's husband.

Eduardo bangs her in the laundry room, Linda's bare ass-cheeks visible in the dust on the dryer lid. He likes to crack the eggs on her ass, and then dip celery, peppers, and cauliflower between her legs.

After their lovemaking he makes a frittata whiles Linda removes toenail polish and repaints her stubby toes with a fresh coat. For fourteen years she's used Mavis's varnish. "Two fat ladies, eighty-eight." Linda forks a mouthful of cauliflower and egg into her mouth and smiles at Eduardo. "Bingo, Bingo, Bingo."

WHERE'S ME DINNER, WOMAN?

Let me take you by the hand and lead you through the streets of London.
—Ralph McTell

1

You shared a house in Harrow and Wealdstone with Frank, Mickey, Ken, and Elaine. The place a cuckoo's nest of oddities. Mickey, Elaine, and Ken were all from the same small town in Northern Ireland, a town containing a large mental institution where it was rumored the entire population had at one time been institutionalized. You heard Ken's maniacal laughter on the tube to Covent Garden one night, his hoots more howler monkey than human being.

Elaine caught your eye, in her fishnets and heels, the leather mini-skirt she wore to work, the same miniskirt Ken borrowed every now and then to wear to the Beehive Pub in Edgware. Ken was the first man you ever saw in make-up. He might have been better at its application than Elaine, and that's something. His lustrous black hair hung to his shoulders and sometimes when he came in the door and went upstairs wearing the heels and miniskirt you mistook him for Elaine.

Mickey and Ken did Kung Fu, drew the dole, and spent all their money on beer and take-out Indian food. Often you flinched as they threw elaborate moves at each other across the sofa in the living room. Mickey was weasel-like, a thin moustache crept across his lip and his eyebrows said more than he ever could. He was mad for Elaine and they'd been together for ten years, since they had been thirteen-year-olds in Ardee.

You laughed when Elaine came home from her workday, after slaving as a secretary in a building site office, and Mickey, fresh from the martial arts studio, beer in hand, would cry from the sofa, "Woman, woman! Where's me dinner?" Funny, she never said a word. Only served Mickey his meals on a tray, with a kiss on the cheek from painted lips.

You watched Nigel come and go, swinging his brolly, three-piece suit and bowler hat, and a job at a bank in the City. He was the only English person in the house. Each month Nigel taped the rent and utilities bills to the bedroom doors and the itemized sheets of paper bore the exactitude of the banker.

Nigel was seeing a woman. When the phone rang in the evening he'd mumble into the receiver. At the appointed time Nigel darted from his ground floor room and opened the front door, ushering his woman into his chamber. You never got a good look at her. She did drive a white VW Beetle.

Now and then some other traveler would stop at the house for a few days, *en route* from Ireland to dig for gold in the streets of London. Nigel's patience wore thin with the steady flow of immigrants surfing the couch. With long vowels accentuated, he'd simply moan, "Oh no! More people?" And after a week they too would be added to the list of billing subjects for rent and utilities.

Kenton Road, number 143. The only address you had in London. Your bedroom so small that if you'd stretched out your arms to yawn, you'd have broken your wrist. And the time the Yugoslav *au pair* you picked up at the Beehive Pub slipped naked into your narrow bed. When you saw her body covered in a thick coat of fur…

2

Birdseye fish fingers, creamed potatoes, Heinz beans, and maybe, just maybe, a slice of buttered toast. All washed down with hot tea, a blessing on you for taking care of your children, missus. Knock once for yes, twice for no. A low card table with a green felt inlay, deck of dog-eared cards, the suits faded and fingered to nothingness.

There was a house up the lane from where we lived, three-story, with a sprawling back garden that seemed to go on forever. It could have been the Garden of Eden, or Gethsemane, but became the garden of criminal intent for our fourteen-year-old minds. The garden was the portal to the brokendown house, its three floors of decayed carpet and abandoned bits and pieces. The owner, we presumed dead, had been an importer of goods from China. One of the upstairs rooms contained boxes of playing cards, diaries, picture frames, fountain pens, and other bric-a-brac—the sort of stuff sold at a stall in the Dandelion Market, but not of sufficient quality for a shop proper.

Every now and then we'd slip in the broken back door and make our way upstairs in the dusty light from the glass over the front door. Whenever the house creaked, its geriatric boards settling into place, we jumped and ran for the corners, listening for footsteps. I was a terrible coward back then and afraid of my own shadow, so to be in that house at all was a daring move. The contents of the house never found their way into my pockets, afraid as I was of my mother finding something and questioning its origins.

The sycamore trees in the wild back garden we climbed all the time, scaling the knotty limbs, pulling ourselves upward toward the sun, to where we could spy on the houses to either side of the abandoned one. Beneath the sycamores was an open area of long grass, the green of which was lighter than that of the leaves of the trees. Summer sunshine poured through the branches, through the latticework of leaves, like a giant tap spilling bright water onto the ground. I lay on the carpet of grass and watched the spangled sunlight through my fingers. Have you ever noticed the click of teeth on teeth when kissed unexpectedly, or when you kiss not knowing what you're doing?

My eyes closed and the sun turned the insides of my lids bright orange, my favorite color. Everything went black and a tongue pushed past my lips, porcelain chinking, the shock of warm flesh in my mouth, the sprouting of doubt in my mind. In a dream state, surrendering. Was it a dream, or really happening to me? Uncertain, I leaned upwards, a fitful lapse in an afternoon nap on a summer's day in my fourteenth year.

This past summer I saw again that house and garden and marveled at how small they'd grown in the meantime. Through the prism of time everything looked so much vaster, so filled with wonder and excitement and uncertainty. Now the house is lived in, the garden manicured, the wall rebuilt where we used sneak through the broken blocks. The thorny bushes and dense undergrowth are gone, and the memory of who kissed me in a dream is broken and splintered on the floor.

3

Limestone. Asphalt. Bitumen. Stones in the road, a telephone pole, silver paint flecks falling away, crude hearts scratched into the steel, fleeting encounters in teenage life are immortalized for the lifecycle of the metal cylinder outside our house. Mam at the door. "Your tea's ready, come on in, now." Sound travels over water. Her voice travels over the tarmacadam ribbon, across the road and up the lane into Hollie's Plant Hire company. Dumpster trucks with slabs of ice, 52 x 42 floes, turn fingers blue, shatter on oil-soaked ground. Perimeter wall is lined with barbed wire, three strands wide, the whole way along. Rust. Orange. Stained and ripped sweaters tell the truth. Over the gate, nightwatchman's caravan. A drop of the hard stuff and he'll not likely come out to investigate random noises. Bolts and tools, girders and spools of electrical wire. Steal what you can. Thievery begins in short pants and ankle socks.

The width of a lane. Size of Wembley Stadium, or Anfield, or Elland Road. Games of three-and-in disrupted by reversing lorries toting giant metal vats. Don't dive on the ground. Trip and stud your palm with stones and bits of glass. Pick them out of the bloody mess. All those years and a window never broke. Not for want of trying. There's Bill stumbling up the road, umbrella-armed, mackintosh wet-spotted, swaying like a sailor off a sea journey. Never been to sea, never been to me. Drunk as a lord. Smell the whiskey at thirty paces. Easy to do given the times. A magpie picks worms out of square lawn, wriggling before disappearing down the gullet. One for sorrow. Seven for a secret. Yes. Never to be told. They're dangerous, right? Secrets. Don't tell. Don't tell. You're in goal now. Skinned knees, bloodied scabs, snotty nose.

SOLEMNITY OF OUR LADY OF GUADALUPE

Santa Fe, NM

Sun spills over adobe wall, the splayed form of an old woman vomiting in her back yard shreds what should be a glorious start to the day, sending me backward reeling. I am unworthy to witness such a moment, having snuck here after the bus dropped me off in the plaza. She's an old teacher of mine and when I heard she was dying I wanted to stop by and see her one last time. We once walked the path to the white cross together in silent meditation. *Penitentes.* From where I sit on my ass, in the dust, a poster peels off the wall:

Clown. Face. Vargas.

The _____ is coming to_____.

In the red earth I am an antic traveler in an awkward state. Once I was a hip young cat with a pair of tortoiseshell Wayfarers stuck in my t-shirt and Marlboros twisted up in the sleeve.

Brooklyn, NY

We had a baby, you see. One hand missing, like a doll discarded after Christmas. Tried to perform the act of good husband. Walked the walk, pushed the puce-green stroller up and down outside our Slope apartment.

Everything I did displeased her. She'd lie in bed, sleepy, the baby's gummed mouth to a milky breast. She'd point out my errors, wordlessly. Her wedding band glinted a destroying ray of energy that made my skin smell of burnt toast. She had super-sensitive smell in those days.

"You need to leave."

Shed like a cat leaving hair on a carpet. The collapse of everything. The time for talk was past. A moment to digest the news, another to stuff some clothes in a bag and vagabond my way out the door and down the road to the underground station. Our time together, cheaply bought in a dive bar, fallen asunder in a Brooklyn morning.

GARDENIA & TAROT

stela

With purpose, relentlessly back and forth, the brush sweeps the grass cuttings from the flags, her hips sway: an afternoon garden dance. The begonia by the door flushes an impatient hue, its energy sickle-scented mythic. In the sun she finds comfort in the wooden handle's rotation, the narrow lines ribbed a thousand times, hands grooved to a familiar shape. The bottle on the hall table migrates from the liquor cabinet all on its own—she has nothing to do with that, she'll later tell the guests. By then the cut blooms will have just the slightest wilt, the evening breeze blowing bedsheets billowed on the washing line's threaded length. Perhaps she'll act like a character in a Tennessee Williams play, all sweaty and inviting in her wrapper dress, the one with the gardenia blossom printed in waves, cigarette smoking into closed air, Van Cliburn on the gramophone. Perhaps.

persia

She wakes undone, body bathed in sweat, bites from his mouth on her torso. She repeats the words: *I am not afraid. I am not afraid.* Frantic, she searches her body for the words, nowhere to be found. Her two eyes, glassed with tiredness, the rolls of sweat come off her in waves. The dream was terrible. Crashed through a windscreen. Broken body. Couldn't survive. No chance. Weary, she makes her way to the kitchen, moonlit and cold. She pours a glass of red, sips and attempts to decipher the maze of the dream. What if he strapped her lightly with his belt? She longs for structure, for order, for enlightenment. He seems a reasonable man. All the signs are there, the eye contact—direct and unnerving. A flood of energy, the way she hopes he'll undress her, the way he works the lab, scientifically. For now, back to bed, and in the morning she'll go to the local tattoo place. Intricate work, along the inside of the ankle, curved and slender as the branch of a willow tree.

FRYDAY, JUNE 17TH, IN THE YEAR 1681

Wooden rafters consumed by fire, the greyed skin smolders in the shit-filled enclosure. Parliament Street, rich in history, in the wee hours, the silence snapped by whiskeyed late-night revellers, "The elephant is on fire!" In flux they attempt to open the doors. Heat and smoke keep them away.

Pained bellows, short then long, the creature batters the walls in vain, as the fire brigade men on their engine wheel into sight. The entire building under cover of smoke and flame, the men pump and spray, the owner curses them on to save his prized exhibit.

At a penny a viewing the elephant is too rich for the blood of most locals, who instead satisfy themselves with a glimpse of the corded trunk as it snakes out the barred window above the thick oak doors. "Bring us to see the effelant," a young girl asks her father, and the poor man shakes his head and rubs her ringlets.

Hungry canines roam the area crazed by the smell of roast flesh. The owner runs a hand against the huge beast's nap, dust rises in a cloud. He shakes his head and wonders if a specialist could save the skeleton for display purposes. A scrap of hide peels away, and with it all pretense.

LOSING MY VOICE

The hall table was an old gramophone. Where the turntable went, a hole surrounded by plush velvet. Small steel needles, nubbed and sharp, lay around the carcass of the HMV cabinet. The speaker, if they called it a speaker back in those days, was set behind hinged doors. Black metal went from wide to narrow, a roadway for the Batmobile I whizzed toward the curve it couldn't get past. When I pushed my Dinky cars though, they disappeared from sight, into the dark uvula. Small fingers strained around the opening, feeling for the lost toys. When the Old Man and Mam moved from our house in the city they got rid of the gramophone cabinet, and with it my childhood, swallowed in the belly of the beast. I wanted to tell them to hang on until my next trip home, but there was a house to empty, a thousand things to do, and the Old Man was failing rapidly. They sold the cabinet to an antiques dealer from town, who shunted it off in the back of a truck, the coffined resting place of lost toys, and my lost childhood. The muffled cry of his master's voice went unheard.

SIXTEEN MAGPIES

On a Tuesday you were prepared for the burial. "He has to face Ben Bulben," she told the undertaker, his dark suit starry-heavened with dandruff, his nose adrip like a leaky bucket. "And make sure his Rosary beads are in his hands so he can recite the fifth sorrowful mystery before the soil drowns out his prayers." The old fellow took the cloth bag with your beads and shook her hand.

Sixteen magpies patrolled the patch of grass behind the house, splitting the soil with their shiny beaks and siphoning earthworms from the wet earth. Your blood and bile suctioned into waste receptacles, your sallow skin pitted and bluing as the sun made its inescapable journey across the Sligo sky.

The grizzled old badger nudged a steel trash can in the yard, spilling the contents with a rattle. You lay on the table, the last vestiges of life draining away, broc's rough tongue cleaning the insides of a tomato soup can.

Your father learned you your animals, giving them the names in Irish, then English. *Easóg*, he said as he gripped the silk-furred stoat in his thick fingers. Your eyes, now glassine, widened with delight as the wild animal squirmed in the old man's grip. *Sionnach*, he said, one night as you watched the russet foxes play on the grass verge of Lough Erne.

The old man died in the war. Heart. He wasn't allowed to enlist. Your mother wrung her hands and wept bitterly for a month of Sundays, and then she took on the business and the register rang like never before.

Undertaker's sleeves were rolled to his elbows, held in place by black elastic bands, you didn't like the cotton-wool swabs he plumped into your cheeks, the dry taste would've made you heave had you been alive. He combed your hair the wrong way. She'd notice at the wake, no doubt. When he knotted your old school tie and cinched it his knuckles rasped the Adam's apple and you could smell the faint aftertaste of sour milk on his breath.

When he rolled you into the viewing room it was bitterly cold and the ripple of chill was in the air. Out the window Ben Bulben was swathed in a late evening wash and the shadow of the sixteen *meaigs* pitted the wall where the coffin rested. She'd be along when the tea was supped and not before. A gurgle of trapped air stirred your jacket and the strains of Carolan's fiddle soothed your restless bones.

WITNESS FOR THE PROSECUTION

Coal fire, the sparks cracking against the guard, a copy of White's Selborne open on the rug, my elbows patterned with the weave of the handmade jumper I got for my birthday this year. Fox, badger, fly-catcher, stone wall, and hedgerow. A small notebook for taking down details. My imagination takes me back to White's East Hampshire wilderness. Upstairs the mattress creaks, the light shade that hangs from the ceiling shakes and an audible coughing seeps through the plaster and boards.

A compass, stub of pencil attached to the other leg, circles intersect and the angles protracted suggest extended periods of heavy rain showers. There's a box under my bed where I stow my untruths. Money stolen from purse and wallet, stained socks and stolen stockings, well-thumbed copies of Ken Follett and Jackie Collins, a candle taken from the corner shop whilst the old lady sliced cooked ham for Mrs. Keogh and her elephantiasis-plagued left leg. The boot and iron makes her look like a failed Frankenstein.

In a glass dish in my parents' bedroom, jeweled animals repose in dimmed light. On Sundays one gets chosen to walk the quarter mile to the church. Lizard or jaguar, oystercatcher or hare? Mass cards for the dead relatives poke out of a chipped vase with pink roses around the rim. Say a prayer for the dearly departed. In the future, a Jewish girl with thick black hair, and a Protestant with an overexposed upper gum-line, will lie with me under the withering stare of the Sacred Heart of Jesus.

Until then, the creatures of the field will take my attention, and the cold linoleum floor of the bathroom will feel my sinful rage. As rain puddles the lane across the road, I watch the upstairs windows of our neighbor's bedroom through ancient field-glasses.She dons the pink lacy nightgown and draws the curtains. In the shift between the two sides coming together I witness the shadow of her breasts backlit by the light from an open door.

HOUSEMATES

A spider lives in the screen door handle. Some nights I come
home and it's cracking knuckles, stretching eight limbs,
preparing for bed. Other nights it snickers at the television, the
tinny voices of *How I Met Your Mother* echoing from the furled
metal handle. If I could invent a device to extract the little
bastard from its hidey hole then life would take on a grand
sweep, much like the battle scenes in Lean's *Lawrence of Arabia.* A
bond between man and arachnid is never a wise one. Friends
say it is a phase I'm going through, a trick of sorts, the kind to
fool my mind into thinking they are not dead. after the shrink
"illuminated" the word grief for me, I declared war on my
neighbor. Webs coated my hand when I brushed the screen,
dark points searched for fleshy skin from its position of safety.
For a time we coexisted, tolerating each the other.

I revel in my surroundings, the familiar wallpaper, the pastels of feeding
swans in tall reeds, the grayish hue of everything thanks to the back-
flow of soot from the chimney. We do not depend on each other—
he, the porch dweller; me, the expressive one living in the splay-
boarded house. To demonstrate my point, I boil the red kettle on the
stove and wait for the whistle to wake me from my evening slumber.

A REFLECTION OF SADNESS
IN THE WATER

CRAVE—A call, the ringing of the bell, the deliverance from all evil. Short of breath, short of sleep, all around is the null set of no escape. On a window a spider, cream-colored, spins silk, weaves time into relentless corridors of space. Cross so many bridges, snap a bloom from a Japanese garden. Etched lines on an already tired face.

SPRAY—A seal bobs between sets. In on the nearing tide, out on the curve of a snapped branch. There is nothing, only the crack of the thick muscle about the heart. See how easily the scalpel penetrates the membrane, exposing the brightness below, and how emotions are carved from bone. Scrimshaw for the twenty-first century.

YIELD—A trident sparks the strangest dreams. In the dark beneath the stage the dust collects in false marbles of air, the stranger's face retaliates against the attempt to coerce it into recognition. Boxes hold beginnings, hold secrets, hold failure in plastic containers, contain the plastic lines that draw marrow from the brittle bone.

LIMP—A key dangles from a chain, useless as a stumped

limb. The door opened is no longer there. A blue envelope with insufficient postage contains a flightless bird, a photocopied flyer from another time. Sinews unravel and separate like watered rope-ends. This insufferable weight presses down on the delicate leaves collected on a fall day in October.

AVOCADO GROVE IN
SIX MOVEMENTS

I

Seals on rocks. The paperwhites bloom. Dog rests on haunches, giant bubbles escape into the warm air. This is a day of rest. Fullness. Little rest. Perhaps wicked, at least *le plus méchant*. Such small mercies, the redemptive pattern of flitting cabbage whites, fragile wings whispering on the rise. We dig and we dig, in search of some other torment. This is the measure, the spoons laid out, the cups washed and waiting.

II

Black widow webs impeach forgotten corners of the property, the haphazardness of the weave a dead giveaway for the locations of ink-skinned demons. Sun tries to break through, a fragmentary look at a summer promised. All greens are not the same—the blood orange leaf and the stag's head fern— shaped and tinted in some maker's guileless hands.

III

Long-handled secateurs, a pair of hurricane lanterns redundant, a small brown frog creeping through the undergrowth. Haze slumps over the foothills this afternoon, red-tailed hawks hidden from view, their sharp metallic cries audible across the busy road. A small boy builds a house for roly-polies, his hesitant steps familiar, yet unknown. Dim the lights and cover the birds for the evening. Tomorrow's another day.

IV

Chamomile—East of the Indies. Splash from a splintered bow, the waves cresting as a downcast moon slumps below the far line. Divinity splays itself out, arms and legs akimbo, wretched battles with a frequent transgressor amount to little, or nothing. If you said, widdershins, I stopped myself from replying.

V

Depth—the perception of something more than what actually exists, the percussive versus the regressive. A limb caught in a vice, the splintering of the tibia, tooth-picked. The writing is no good, the hallucination of a state of awareness that might not help in the long run. Sitting could make a difference, the posture corrected, the straightened spine. Limp away to a corner and enshroud yourself.

VI

Sculpt—the ricocheting of stone on stone, wood on water, a curled set of letters, emptied graves, a woodshed set back from the road. Three calico cats shunt their fur against the siding, burgundy eyes diamond the lease line. Always the memory of angry words, curses on linoleum floors, the harsh tone as bitter as a halved lemon licked. Everything still in the lee of the mountain.

MERCURY RETROGRADE

I am running away from myself. In bed at night, the heat makes me sweat, saltwater skin, my limbs tremble from the nightmare. No one was where they were supposed to be; not the office administrator, nor the rabbit that lives under the trailer, nor the plastic statue of the Virgin of Guadalupe that usually sits on my desk. It's all about timing, I tell myself. The horoscope says not to sign any contracts for three weeks, and with Mercury at such an awkward angle to my index finger, I'm not going to quibble. Not that I'll stay silent forever. Even though the silence is where my father's remains rattle about in that expensive coffin, I'm more comfortable in the vacuum of words than I am without. I've found ways to slay my progress, to retard the possibilities, in the same way the shy girls huddle around handbags on the dancefloor. There's safety in numbers— their wagons circled, targets for lone wolf lovers searching for weaknesses. There I am, cloak fastened, like a bantamweight in a boxing ring, twig arms aloft, ready for the fight. My timing must be off, because there's a wet patch in the bed where the piss goes. The TV ads suggest cures for incontinence, sporty men and women doing their thing with freedom, safe in the knowledge they won't wet their pants mid-stroke or mid-kick. Flight is the result of my freakout, the urge to run, to head for the exit, to find that neon sign with the text brightly-lit above the chained door.

SPREADING FROM THE FALSE FLY

I sleep on my back and the light fixture showers my face with petals from the dried flowers we brought back from my father's grave. The day he died, a light freeze covered the neglected lawn outside the ward window; the blades curved with the weight of the frozen water, as if they were the discarded ribs from Sunday's roast. A bowl of fruit sat beside his steel-framed hospital bed, despite three weeks of unconsciousness. He unpeeled a greenish banana, looked at me with his good eye, and said I wasn't to feel guilty for not being there when he died.

"Fear no more the heat of the sun," my teacher said in our literature seminar. My father stood ankle-deep in the cold Atlantic water, trunks speckled with salt residue, his cheeks puffed out, body intact and goosebumps all over his bare skin. I chose to ignore his attempts to communicate with me, the subtly-put advice he tried to give me falling into the carpet. And after the class ended, I checked my phone messages and learned how a series of mini-strokes had left him without color and with one foot in Charon's ferry.

After a long flight from LAX to Heathrow the pay phone's tiny screen flashed as the coins dropped. Three rings.

My mother's voice. "Ah, he died this morning at six, as the sun was coming up." I sat among the haphazard travelers and their carry-on bags waiting for the connecting flight to Dublin. Three cups of strongly-brewed Costa coffee; and in the cup, the spiraling sand dunes and sharp-edged marram grass, summer holidays in thatched cottages, the memory of his laugh.

What I remember of the drive to the funeral home was the dead bugs embedded in the car's radiator grille—moths, butterflies, an early wasp, and a mayfly. My father tied his own flies for fishing—a real knack. By the banks of the River Boyne he wristed the bamboo rod back-and-forth, the soft ripples spreading from the false fly, ever outward, to where he stood in his waders at the water's edge, dead at eighty-three, but still unknowing.

THE DING HEARD AROUND
THE UNIVERSE

On a cool October evening in 1971, we gather at the electricity pole to recreate the Jerry Quarry/Muhammad Ali fight. Jimmy Deegan is Quarry, and Danny O'Hanlon is Ali (because he is black Irish and has no father). Ten of us link arms to make a boxing ring and Jimmy's brother, Enda, dings his bicycle bell to signal the start of the fight.

Danny makes his entrance beneath the arm I have linked with Leslie Kennedy, his curly hair brushing my sleeve. Jimmy tears across the ring and lands a clatter on his rival's chin. "what'd you do that for," Danny cries.

Jimmy ignores the question and does his imitation of the Ali shuffle, his brown brogues scuffing the tarmacadam floor of the ring. Another swing and his fist lands close to Danny's eyebrow. There's blood, and Danny turns away from his nemesis. The crowd chants, "Ali, Ali, Ali!" Jimmy raises his closed fists to the rain-clouds.

The bell rings for the end of the round and the two fighters take their seats on folded anoraks in opposite corners of the ring. Along the tops of the railings, my mother's roses sway in the wind, their pink and red faces filling the nosebleed seats on the last day of our Indian summer.

The bell chimes again and the boys shuffle around the makeshift circle. Danny's face is guarded by his two curled hands, and Jimmy stalks him like a starved seagull chasing a rind of fat on a windy day.

THE SKY IS A PRAIRIE

After my heavy dinner of spaghetti and two bottles of red wine, the rat crawls inside the walls, its feet rattling, scratching, its very existence the definition of torture. Without a moon, the sky is a prairie, widespread dark. Bait proves useless, the poisoned pellets gray and dissolve where they lie. I fantasize about the rat, how I shall create a noose from a shoelace and place it over an opening in the breeze-blocks, wait in the silence for a shark-eared head to poke through, and in a flash tighten its neck in a death grip. But there is no sign of the rat, only the approach of bad weather. Clouds cabbage, white and massive in the night. After I comb the perimeter of the property— my flashlight waking daisies from their sleep, mushrooms with caps bowed, the dew-drenched bench under the apricot tree—the memory of a word rattles me. Crisp. A verb: *to make brown and crisp by heating*. Tomorrow, when the sun breaks frees from its moorings on the far side of the hilltop, I shall wire each metal grid where the rat might enter the wall space, and run a current through the grille until nothing remains but the dried, charred corpse of the bastard.

THE TEARING OF SKIN

On a spar of telephone pole. A mouse in its paws. Is it playing, or is it survival? A cascade of feathers, buff, red, white, the tearing of skin. This was not something I witnessed in Ireland. Terra-cotta earth, the white cross, walk the way of the penitents. A white band, yellow backswept, the snow riddles the cracks of the far-off *Sangre de Cristo,* and frosted windows fade to nowhere.

That was then, this is now: a carpet of muted color, the spread pages of an old notebook, ideas, schematics. An evening sun breaks its brittle rays on the gable-end of the house and a russet coyote pads past my window, bound for the chicken coop. Most days I don't have the energy to spin fabulist passages of an Irish childhood.

Once upon a time the man traveled from town to town, seeking a welcoming hearth, a stool to sit upon, and a bowl of steaming food, before telling his stories. There's perfection in the arched sunflower as it bends its head earthward, flowers dead, the seeds ready to spread across the earth. My hand stayed by a single thought.

CRUMBS OF DARKNESS

In the space beneath the stairs where the nanny devours her children, the crumbs of crushed femurs and clavicles litter the floor. She is alien, she is a thousand years old, she speaks with a Flemish accent, and her skin is aquamarine. When we sleep in the afternoon the trouble brews. The dream causes me to thrash about in the cot, arms waving, beads of sweat on my brow, eyes gummed shut. When she reaches in and attempts to restrain me, I am startled by the ice-pick fingers that wrap about my thin bones. She hums a tune, a merry wedding tune, as she shoves me into the pantry beneath the carpeted stairs. I want my mommy and daddy, not this child-eater. They are not here, not since the clinical trials began. She told me their number had been called, and I cried for the longest time. Now, the darkness and the crumbs and the small, polished teeth tickle my skin, and the last strains of the wedding song fade into the world.

ORWELL LODGE HOTEL, ROOM NO. 8

Smell of burnt popcorn. Sky the color of pencil lead. Flakes fell, plump and silent. Down the hill past the hospital, across the frozen Dodder. Car tires slushed through the collected snow at the pit of the pendulum by the small kiosk that sells ice cream in the springtime. Sight blocked, her hand on mine, first gear to climb to the top. On the right, the hotel, lights blurred in the falling snow, the sign heavy with frosting. No further, no point, home too far away. We parked in the lot, signed the register, not a married couple: she, barely out of teenage life; me, heading to the first speed limit of my life. The heavy carpeted stairs, plush, red hues, some dark blue in there, too.

From outside the strange light turned the room aglow. In a bed with an inordinately large mattress we undressed and slipped between washed sheets, crisp, white, dry. Her small cold feet touched mine and I withdrew from the contact. In the glow of the streetlight, the digital alarm clock rednumbered the minutes to morning, we closed distance, two springs intertwined. Spread on the crisp pillowcase, flamed hair fanned out, trace of *Anaïs Anaïs*. A haloed sinner in the Orwell Lodge Hotel, room number 8.

BONE

A furrow of metal pieces hold my skull together, inexpertly riveted in place by a disaffected nurse practitioner. How did it happen, she asked. The truth, unknown, the fiction a woven mat of dark rooms and ill-placed furniture. Even as I made my way to the parking lot, the bone revolted from the metal, the clear fluid gelled on the wound, and the low moon hung ashamedly in the bare trees. Strength through prayer, a fallback position, the unspoken cure-all for my family afflictions. Spare a few coppers? the tinker in the blanket asked at the hospital gate, the mummified baby hugged to her chest. My left eye fell down to the bottom of the socket and rebounded shakily for a few seconds. In my pocket, my fingers rubbed lint and thread together, a complete absence of coin.

TAROT I

The underlying card is death—change, transformation, upheaval. Cross that with so many sevens, magical, dreamland someplace. A shattered bone; femur held in place with stainless steel implants. Sea crashes against a sloping cliff and someone scurries about below, telling me to take the same path as they do. A girl with a Scottish accent has brought me to this place. I am unsure whether she's a lover, or not. In the night, the night, the clouding over of bare sky lends the place the look of a lunar landscape. Fellow travelers are unknown to me, strangers, other dreamers brought to the same locale, given no choice. Moving away from the shore, moving from the issue bursting from earth, moving in the direction of the horizon, somewhere between the ripples and the feeding fish. Second to go, the shock of siblinghood, one man's murder, a brother with a cleft palate and three fingers on his left hand. "It's really, really pretty," the Scottish girl says, with a laugh, as the silver flickers over the sea. She has a reputation—short hemmed and sassy—centered down the middle of the page. Does she know the world she's entered into, or is her brogue too thick to make a difference? Over there on the slimed rocks—an old man whose pajama pants are frayed nerves—the sheen of motor oil flickers bluegreenorange.

TAROT II

The gloom, the gloom, a falling card, face-up, Hierophant. Long bones, thigh most likely. In God we thrust. The lack of a fund makes the opening up of the year a mystery and a place of fear. Across the road the grind of machinery, man working on floorboards perhaps. The green house has new floors, sanded nice and even, smooth and broken in by the renter and her daughter. Spread: the King of Swords, Magician, Hanged Man, strength, King of Pentacles. Death. Reversal: Queen of Swords, High Priestess, Cernunnos the Stag Lord, the Lady. What will it feel like to drive out of New Orleans and know the chapter is finished? Out the window the orange flag flutters weakly in the breeze, a proclivity to over-interpretation. A yellow plastic chair on a green lawn, the sun filtering through ancient branches. How much blood can a mosquito withdraw at one time? The bees crawl around the outside of the hive in the darkness. Are they sleepwalking, or searching for meaning in their lives? A stegosaurus stenciled on a steel girder spanning a slow-moving body of water. Four men fish in the water for the corpses of dogs or cats using bread torn from a loaf for bait.

NOT ENOUGH

The being enough, the water boiled, the leaves soaked until flavor releases, and never enough for the only failures are the sharp pangs of a heart attack waiting to be enough on a fine day in June, the paperwhites abloom, the bees radar-like about the blossoms, and enough then will be not enough for the fell hand to swoop from on high and deliver the ripped envelope bearing the news of the not enough of hardened arteries and unpaid bar bills, the scattered pencils from a boy's satchel, and the not enough of his teacher's lonely flat on the outskirts of a town quite like your own, but not enough like the map of the human body contained in the shallow space between skin and bone, and the riparian in the tall trees, the not enough of flesh rent from bone, the same bone that made a needle to darn with when the world was not enough old to know the various sorrows to come, and the shadow of the magpie on the pavement outside the window as the not enough day goes into night and the streetlights cast not enough in the shadows where the youths kiss and whisper not enough to make a difference to the unhappy lives they will fall into when not enough education and not enough birth control leads to a life that is not enough, not now, not then, and certainly not to come.

ILLUMINATING EVERY FEAR

I

The spot from where it will appear, this great thing I am waiting for out there, in the fields, in the streets of some unknown city; just like I was, or still am, out there wandering lost in some wilderness at five or six years old. Displacement has rendered me a missing soul. There's something I seek like a buried jewel in Varanasi. I leave my body sometimes and go in search of this fabled object, this clod-covered piece of ephemera that will put my soul at rest. I've seen it before it has to be said, in my father's house when I was a little boy. My mother polished this treasure every week, gently handling it, rubbing its bumpy surface with a cloth. Perhaps she has the answers today, sitting in her kitchen, lonely, abandoned by her brood, smoking a cigarette as the black clouds rumble across the window and drop sheets of gray water on the land?

II

It is coming. She is certain. I am less certain but know there must be a shift in the way these things are approached. Believe in the possibility of it and it can take place, open a weal in your flesh, small enough to place a finger or two, and know there lies the entryway for the approaching good fortune. Speak the words, words of love, of life, of healing: abandon the words of death, of corruption, of impotence. I have zipped my jacket up to the neck, pulled the collar around my large, pinkish ears, narrowed my eye slits against the swirling sand as it whips up off the beach and takes to the air dervish-like. Choppy water, the dolphins are far off shore, or far below the violent waves, only the stubborn gulls stand at the shoreline, huddled together, bundled in their feathers, staring at the fierce water, every now and again one of them allowing the wind to catch itself and propel it down the beach like a paper kite in a hurricane. When the wind tumbles them in the gusts and hurtles them along, are they afraid, or do they revel in the thrill of the movement?

III

Nowhere on the seascape can I find what I seek. It's not there yet, if it's ever going to be there. I might not be in the right place. She didn't speak of places geographic, only of those places of the soul, the fiercely buttressed inside vaults, dark cobwebs hanging from the eaves, a faint chink of light cutting the pitch like a scalpel, illuminating every fear I've ever felt. The cards pointed to the void—Knight of Cups, the Queen of Cups, the Magician, the Hanged Man—and my father who could die tonight while my five-year-old body lies awake in the dark listening, waiting for his breathing to stop, and the mourning to begin. Am I going to grow up and fail? How will I make the change from child to adult without the map that's buried off on some barren headland somewhere? I try to sleep.

DEW ON THE STALK

Never saw it coming, the peregrine out of the deep blue sky, outstretched legs, talons a-glint, the young snakes oblivious. This is the order of things, how the pyramid works, the chain of command, a glass ceiling of Linnaean exactitude. Look back, through the door with the chipped paint and the broken lock.

Once, the door opened onto an ordered field, an orchard, rows of apple trees, cookers, granny smiths, beauty of baths, day-old snail silver tracked here and there. Under pressure, the bank tightened its grip, the trees wildened, tall grass sprang up where before order ruled. In the Carmelite convent the nuns sang *Terce* and the bishop let out his belt a notch, the dried egg yolk yellowed in his whiskers.

In the field, unseen by most, the stoat licked first the left, then the right paw, fastidious, aware of every small movement. Soft underbelly, the hairs stiffened by its saliva, both eyes black beads, the writhing snake caused the stoat no sense of loss, or dismay. Instead, ablutions over, the animal turned around and chose a path through long grass to where an earthen burrow opened in the shade of a wall. Gone, not forgotten, much in the manner of a late-morning dream, one of those that remains in the memory for fleet moments, before the mind awakens fully and the dream recedes like dew on the stalk.

Over the tabernacle, the masochism of perpetual motion, fingers to forehead, to breastbone, to heart, to ribcage, all the missing children running around playing hide-and-go-seek in the church grounds. Plainsong, the apple of a mother's eye, straining to count to thirty. Possible that the house next-door is full of ghosts, handwringing, whispering, colluding specters of motes, transmigrating from rotting flesh to fleeting view in a window. The finial should have told the story, but the ivy grew and spoiled the clue. Tallow lamps lit the rooms at night, the shiver of curtain, the flicker of white, empty steps on broken boards.

Arabesques turned in air, midnight show-time, no attendees, save the broken chairs, the dusty tables, a lone rat hugging the wainscoting, the dancers unwatched, uncared for. If the peregrine flew at night between the apple trees, wing-whispers and trained eyes, no creature would avoid its sleepless scrutiny. Percussive angels, feasting on moted souls pass one another by and nod politely, the hidden meaning clear to all but the soulless. And in a corner, an abandoned violin slumps against the wall, strings frayed and unfingered.

بيضـــــاء بومـة / INTIFADA

We gathered the solution in ten-gallon drums, all the time working on our technique, moving towards an exact science, wherein the "material" created would cause the greatest damage and loss of life. The recipe came from Jer's grandfather, from the old days, when he and his buddies traipsed about the countryside in the night, setting fire to police stations, and watching from the hedgerows as the poor, flustered guards ran about trying to quell the flames with buckets of water and gravel.

These days, we are sharper tacks, and apply techniques gleaned in foreign lands, in desert regions, days and nights that'd melt the face off you with the heat, and then the cold. Words I learned here: intifada, hanum, بيضـــــاء بومـة. You were a widow at twenty-nine. Twins—girls, primary school-goers. When they were at school I would sneak into your house and drink hot, sweet tea, and then make love to you, the sweat sheening on your lean, brown skin. They liked the sweets I brought from home, the Jelly Babies made them laugh. You refused to say goodbye when I went home.

I seal the drums for transportation to the hollowed-out underground caves where we store them until we are ready to make a statement. I'm the one who keeps track of the locations on an old ordnance survey map of the region. The last time we planted one it was a complete flub; something about the switch, a loose wire, and the bastards were able to drain it safely. Next time, more careful, no drugs amongst the brothers. We'll bring the intifada.

MY MOTHER'S HANDS

When the Virgin Mary appeared to me in the quarry, I was full to the gills. Sitting on the ruins of an old Singer sewing machine, I'd been inclined to have a tipple, but after a spin or two of the old flywheel, I'd emptied half the goddamned bottle. I remember wiping off the smudge of fingerprint, and through the greenish lens of the bottle a shape blurred into flesh. I reckon you'd think I was some sort of crank, but I swear, in those blue robes, she was true. A tingle went through my fingers and the bottle hit the soft grass and the whiskey spilled into the dry ground. She bent over and wiped the neck with the sleeve of her gown.

"You remind me of my son," she said, swallowing a mouthful, her accent clipped, proper. "He had hands like yours, calloused, honest. I miss him, you know."

What do you say to the Virgin Mary? I reckon she must have liked me well enough, to be talking to me. "Ma'am, I hear he was a good man, is all."

She hobbled a ways, close to me, held out both hands, like you see her do in the statues. When I touched those hands I noticed how like my mother's they were. She had the same crooked, arthritic bones. We sat together for a while, watching grave crows return for the evening over the tops of the tall cork oaks, not really saying much to each other.

GENEROSITY

There is a stumbling that takes place, an unsettled movement by foot, from the southernmost corner of the orchard where the blasted well rusts in the hot sun, to the northern portion where the clapboard house is situated. Everything worthwhile has gone now, nothing left but the flakes of memory that make up the stain on the antimacassar.

The dead of night is when I feel it most. The broken veins in my cheeks stopstart, stopstart, an almost invisible pulsing. It takes quite some time to settle into the valley in the center of the mattress. Even though she's been long dead, the rocker remains the same, the soft roll created by years of marriage cemented by cold nights and a lack of central heating.

Worthwhile labor takes place in the orchard, stumping the trees, grafting the new young limbs carefully into place, set into the raw grooves cut by penknife. The finch's beak is a bright color, its tiny claws gripping the fallen branch. The boots hurt my feet, even though I soaked them in water and stuffed each foot with a month's worth of the local newspaper.

I enjoy the keeping of secrets; the way the whiskey bottle hangs by a twist of steel wire in the well, the pallor of the skin under her sagging breasts when I touched her, cold, the morning she died, the leaving of money in the pages of library books for strangers to find. She never did enjoy my getting drunk, and occasioned to tell me so on a frequent basis.

Troubles evaporate quicker than expected and the weight of the work pains my lower back. Old age has set its stall out in my bones, the ripening of organs, the groaning of joints, the streetseller's cries to market. Against the roughness of the tree trunk I undermine any remaining hope by recalling how she bought lemons at market and ignored our own fruit trees.

ALL THIS LIFELONG LATER

A world I have known and forgotten now, all this life-long later. Coman's and Murphy's pubs, set opposite each other like castles on a chessboard, the traffic lights separating the file between them. Always the sour smell of spilled porter seeping up from the cellar grates on the footpath. Those pubs saw a great deal of drink consumed in their day. My old man used limp up the road for a "short and a tall"—a pint of Guinness and a glass of Power's Gold Label whiskey. He'd cross at the primary school, red-bricked and low roofed, and continue on up past the Motor Factors where the Gem Gem sweet-shop used sit. In the Gem Gem, barley sugar, kola cubes, fruit salad, blackjacks, pineapple cubes. A penny went a long way there. At Christmas the window filled with Roses' circular tins, selection boxes, and, of course, Hadji Bey's Turkish Delight. The sweet squares of soft candy were embalmed in a bed of powdered sugar, and stuck to the roof of your mouth long after consumption. Later, by Harrison's Row on the other side, where the knacker's kids lived, Dad would look in on Ward the cobbler and have a word. Ward was a man the color of shoe leather, with a wild thatch of frizzy hair and large eyeglasses, always with dirt beneath his fingernails from shoe dye, or tannins. He'd tap nails with a small-headed hammer, tacks so sharp and shiny they glinted in the dark of his shop. The antique shop was next door, a long shopfront, big windows with divans and candelabras, and always a sleeping marmalade cat in the window, seeking the morning sun. The road was narrow—curving at the small teashop where a pound would buy a pot of tea for two and a couple of sausage rolls—a curse to buses, being too narrow for the tilting double-deckers, only the low single-deckers were routed this way. Fogarty's was where we got vegetables and the daily messages. The grocer looked like a carrot, all red tufts of hair and dark skin, lined with deep wrinkles in which the dirt of the shop collected each day. Across the way the gourmet shop sold stinky French cheeses and olive tapenade, things we had no use for. When we went in there for some tidbit or other, we invariably turned our noses up at the aroma that today would have me in clover. Deveney's off-license was an Aladdin's cave of alcohol and cigarettes. Sent on an errand for a naggin of whiskey, the shop assistants would sell to us as ten-year-olds, wrapping the flat bottle in brown paper and warning us to "be careful not to drop it on the way home." I suppose I feel a sense of loss when I remember such moments from home, as if the sands in the hourglass of life are passing more rapidly through the narrow neck these days. Perhaps the top of the glass contains the sands of home and the ones collecting in the bottom are my life here in America. How many grains remain up above? Will someone right the hourglass when the sands finally run through and the top chamber empties completely?

HER SHOULDER AN ENIGMA

There's a hum in the air near the end of the property line where the neighbor's floodlight gutters orange onto our lawn. Truthfully, it's not a lawn, rather a presence of green stalks, cropped close by the wandering goat that circles the neighborhood gardens at will.

Once, my mother told me a story about a time the family had nothing to eat except a roast goat my father stole from the parish priest's land. "God forgive your father, but the hunger drove him to it." She spoke of him with a tenderness I never knew possible. The wisp of cobweb from the outside toilet draped her shoulder like an enigma, as she told me this. The old man often said he'd "bomb the bloody jakes," but nothing ever happened. Must have been low on his list of priorities, what with fifteen children to feed and clothe.

Ma refused to go to the Vincent de Paul, and instead relied on her eleven brothers and sisters to supply the brood with clothing and shoes. She was a proud woman, always strode through town with her head high, despite the line of debtors from the butcher's shop next-door to the little corner shop beside the church hall.

My loneliness stems from losing the tip of my tongue in

a strange accident when I was five. Ma had flipped open a can of potted meat and didn't I grab the tin and lick the pinkness. The lid hung off the can and overcome with hunger, I didn't see the sharp edge and lost a good portion of flesh. My blood mixed with the ham and I sat on the floor and cried.

Ma hugged me tight and had the presence of mind to put the severed tip in a handkerchief and bundled me out the door and up the road to the vet's office, for we couldn't afford the real doctor. I sat on a small wooden chair in the vet's waiting room. Eventually, the big old Austin Cambridge pulled into the garage next-door, and we saw the vet himself stride by the waiting-room window.

In the office, he grinned at me, and gave Ma a broad wink. "I had to snip the nutmegs off old Johnny Brophy's stallion. Wasn't it riding everything God put in front of it, the hoor!" he said, laughing.

Ma reddened, and held the hanky out to him.

"Did you cut your little pecker off?" he said to me.

I shook my head and gripped Ma's skirt tight as he reached into the dark of his Gladstone bag.

THE DEPTHS OF THE STEEL VAULT

Nothing to it, I thought, as I stood outside the rear entrance to the maternity hospital. Sidle up to the dumpster, find the bag containing the afterbirth, dash home, stick it in the oven and bake for thirty minutes at 325. Parking was the problem. I wedged the Geo Metro between a recycling dumpster and a stone bollard, waited for a few minutes, saw the nurse across the way shuffle towards the back entrance.

I told myself it wasn't dirty, *per se*, to steal the afterbirths of some worthy, fat, ten-toed-and-fingered newborn from the depths of the steel vault. I was bearing out what my folks had always said, that I was one tough piece of work. The home life they afforded me was hardly anything to crow about. I spent a great deal of time hauling buckets of coal from shed to living room, day in, day out. The old man was a lazy fuck. Horse racing, or greyhounds on cable TV. Always bitching at the old lady, who was quiet as a mouse. She had married into her nightmare after all. Who knew a welder from Essen would have been so mean to her?

Into the dumpster I went, ass over elbow, and ended up sliding about in a pool of sick. Just my fucking luck, I cursed, hoping no one was in earshot. When I got to my knees I discovered my hand had squashed a dead mouse, its eyeballs hanging on sinewy threads from the sockets. No broken bones, it appeared, after I checked myself over once or twice. At least I could still search for the placenta now I was knee deep in the shit. Here I was, making lemonade from the lemons of life.

THE LAST DANCE

A slap on the face, the smell of alcohol, tights with runs in them, a country girl at heart. Her flat is in the city, close to the American Embassy, the odd-shaped building across the road from the Horseshow House. Crepe bows in shop windows, the president dead, soon to be buried. These are the darkest days of the year, the fumbling about in the bathroom for an elusive mascara brush, the rushed cup of Nescafe in the mornings. The glass is half an inch thick, frosted, obliterating the passing traffic in a blur of motion.

After *the last dance, last chance for love,* the national anthem signals the slow walk home, or somewhere else. *You'll have a drink, won't you?* she asks. Bushmills. Good country girl. The hair is loosened, shoulder-length, the lipstick patchy and kissed away. Two glasses. *To hold me, to scold me.* In the kitchen, we kiss, her mouth cigarette-scented, mixed with Estee Lauder's finest. She bites my lip and laughs.

What the fuck did you do that for? Then the slap. Eyes water. *You're fucking nuts.*

Go on, she says. *You like it. I can tell.*

The whiskey warms my stomach and we collapse on the divan. The buttons are too thick for the narrow slits. Her brassiere is functional, not at all sexy. *Can you fill my appetite?* The remains of a steak-and-kidney pie rest in oil-stained paper. My hand shivers static from the nylon tights, her laughter sharp as cracking ice. Through the hanging beads separating us from the kitchen, the radio plays on. *I'm so, so bad,* she croons, her fingers wrapped about my hair, her tongue wetting my earlobe.

In the bedroom, a music box with a tiny ballerina pirouettes as the key unwinds to Tchaikovsky. A blow to the head, she straddles me, her horse-riding thighs trapping me. *'Cause when I'm bad, I'm so, so horny,* she mouths, the Carlow accent mocking the words. I'm tongue-thick, the whiskey working its magic. The flat palm catches me open-mouthed, and the split lip leaks blood into my mouth.

Let me up, I say.

She only laughs, wriggles her torso on top of me, and sings, *Come on baby, let's dance tonight.*

SPLINTERED

River water bubbles from my mouth, dirty gray liquid cascading over stones rough and smooth. I came to this place at the narrowing of the year, a hike through the slush-filled fields to clear my head and prepare for the year ahead. In the stream, a discarded tin can, and inside the jigsawed remains of a small trout. Its scales rainbow in the winter light, its jaws wordlessly mouthing for last week's oxygen. From the top of the bluff the world unfolds, only the metal framework of a radio antenna corrupts the view. At its point, a red bulb pulses energy into sky, catching falling flakes in dangerous light. A bobcat plods hard soil far below. I am as quiet as the corpsed fish. The cat's paw touches empty air, and all that hurts breaks the surface. I stumble, smooth soles failing on frozen ground. My head bangs the rock as my descent begins. Gritted teeth splinter into ice-shards. At the bottom, discarded hardware from a lost grocery store blooms from the ground. The metal trolley grid makes of my cheek a chessboard.

THREAD OF RED CHEESECLOTH

I'd arrived with only the severance money from a crap job, the notes wrapped in an elastic band. The tour guide from the travel agency told me to guard it well, Crete not being the safest of spots. Frost, *The Collected Poems*, that's what I was reading. I'd walk out to a deserted beach every morning and strip down to my trunks, spread the towel on an abandoned wooden deck, and memorize "The Road Not Traveled." The black buzz-buzz insects terrified me. The first night, I slept in the back room of my rented apartment, more cell than room, the drone of the lonely mosquito played as background music.

You commented on my book that first morning as I ate breakfast of yogurt and fruit at the small restaurant next to my apartment. You loved Frost, not the "Stopping by Woods" Frost, but the one who wrote, "Out, Out, the buzz-saw snarled." Your friend, American, sipped black coffee and read the *International Herald Tribune*. Later, I swam offshore, the sun scorching, and threw my Speedos to the beach in an act of bravado. When the German couple arrived and sat on low chairs on the gravelly sand, I had to pick my way carefully up the beach to my trunks, modesty covered by my hands. I needn't have worried, as the woman shed her swimsuit like a rubber glove and, bare-arsed, immersed herself in the warm blue water. She called to her husband to join her, but he tilted his hat over his eyes and grunted.

That evening we sat at adjacent tables, moussaka for me, pink calamari for you, the American squeezing lemon and scowling when you invited me to join you on the bus to the Palace of Minos the next morning. When I left you were ordering another jug of retsina and kissed my cheek. I stole a look at the cleft between your breasts and slipped along the cobbled street to my dark apartment.

To Knossos by bus, we sat together by the door, the driver a heavily mustached man with an oil-stained Panama hat jaunty on his head. Of kings and dolphins we talked, and of your small flat in Hampstead Heath, with its oblong windows that opened at street level. I pulled you into the shadows of an amphora as tall as you, and kissed your open mouth. The cheesecloth shirt you wore felt good to the touch, the tied strings of your bikini peeking from the collar. Goat cheese, garlic, and olive oil, your breath a picnic in a field of sunflowers. You couldn't, mustn't, you said. He was your sort-of boyfriend, a visiting Rhodes Scholar from Pennsylvania. Retsina overload kept him in bed while we explored the labyrinth of King Minos. I told you how I loved the crooked way you smiled, and your perfect toenails, painted eggshell, like the mosaic tiles of vaulting girls. When your hands pushed me away, a long thread of red cheesecloth had twined about my finger, as if it were the entryway to the hidden chambers of your heart.

Back in the village, I locked the door to the apartment and lay naked on the bed, the fan creaking overhead, the lone mosquito droning like a live current somewhere out of sight. The place had its own smell, peculiar, yet necessary, a scent that lodged in my memory these past thirty years. Oldness, emptiness, olive oil-stained wood, whatever it was, it has traveled the years with me, a stowaway from another life. The cracked tile on the floor shifted when I padded barefoot to the shower, flushed the exposed negative of your kiss in cold water and felt the wall vibrate from the tolling of the church bells from the Orthodox church up the street.

Mantilla-covered ladies stepped up the uneven stones to the chapel. I followed them inside, the space lit by gilded chandeliers, walls hung with time-worn frescoes. Kneeling in prayer, I felt like an intruder, among all these dark-skinned old people, faces nut-brown, like a swarm of humans halfway through the process of morphing into squirrels. In Greek they prayed, the words echoing in the old walls, as I made my own silent prayer to my own personal God, to remove the American from the island and allow you to fall in love with me. Empty vessel, empty prayer, the feeling of outsider sent me away from the solemnity of the mass. Instead of prayer, I hiked the narrow path uphill to the *kafenion* and sat with my book of poems open on the table. On the blue water a small vessel puttered toward the leper island, sunburned tourists leaning over the gunwales, seeking the balm of the spumed wake. I pictured you with the American, a lanky young man with black-framed glasses, and a tuft of hair over his forehead., arm-in-arm, the taste of my mouth still on your lips.

Back in the apartment I rested on the bed, the jingle of the mattress the only music in the humid Cretan evening. The bouzouki players wouldn't play until later, when the tourists were sitting around the tables of the tavernas dotting the seafront. The scent of the Hawaiian Tropic tanning oil from where my fingers rubbed your neck was still on my fingers as I dropped my Speedos to the floor. In time to the humming mosquito, my eyes squeezed tight, I touched myself while the shadows swallowed the last of the day's sunlight.

The oystercatcher spun towards the ocean, its eye a salt jewel, its beak slicing air, and the sky a riot of white clouds filled with the next day's rain. I wore the scarf I'd bought in Plaka, from a stranger, a woman beneath an olive tree, smoking a pipe, the fine wisps drifting into the orchard. I went to give it to you, but another couple was in your place, nothing left of you save the faint scent of garlic and tanning oil.

SKULL OF A SHEEP

You are in a car speeding through Dublin towards the West year after year the journey uncoils past the same landmarks Kilmainham Jail strapped to a chair bullet to the brain on by the Rowntree Mackintosh factory where the black and yellow and orange and red fruit gums and sugar-covered pastilles spit out of humming machines through the streets by the Deadman's Inn where in the last century the cellar was a makeshift mortuary for corpses carried in from stagecoaches and a little further up the road the Spa Hotel perched on a hillside like some angular magpie on a branch and out the road we whizz by the Hitching Post and the Salmon Leap Inn into the country the green sward dotted with black-and-white cows cudding the grass tripartite stomachs long-lashed eyes lulled creatures the spire of the church in Kinnegad visible well before driving into the narrow-streeted town and Da stopping to wet his whistle at Jack's Roadhouse and Eamonn's butcher's shop next door where we bought beef and lamb and turkey at Christmas and on towards the West through pastureland with the distillery and the castle and Da's cry of "Goodbye Ireland I'm off to Kilbeggan" and Horseleap aptly named as in a

blink the town disappears and with it the hillside graveyard
where our ancestor's bones lie and into Moate of the widest
main street in Ireland site of our family's bitterest defeat at
the hands of bank manager and solicitors aided and abetted
by the Sisters of Mercy later reputed to be torturers and
abusers in habits and all wringing hands and uttered prayers
Hail Holy Queens and the family business on the right the
long low building and Da's mutters of regret and Mam saying
bad luck go with it and out past Brendan Grace the vet's
house on the left and the sight of him with his bordissio
ready to geld the lily-white testicles of young boys through
tree-lined arbors into Athlone—Mam's town and the
narrowed streets houses falling in on one another the Prince
of Wales Hotel and across the road Uncle Tom's shop and
the room where you remember seeing Granny in the bed
the lights dimmed camphor and mothballs and the mutinous
Shannon out the window at the bottom of the slipway and
off across the river by Custume Barracks and Lough Ree
where Mam as a small girl waited in the rushes for swans
and salmon and Lecarrow and Castlerea until the day
stretches towards evening and tired voices recite Hail Marys
and Our Fathers and the Rosary beads clack in the stuffy
car and Da berates Mam for not teaching us our prayers
and is it heathens she's raising and the air of summer full of
ire and Castlebar turns towards Westport and the Wild
Animal Park we never visit disappears as the Atlantic coast
gapes in front of us and Rosturk fades behind us and over
the humpy bridge where Loftus the postman will take flight
years later on his Honda fifty and wind up dead in a ditch
the motorcycle bent in half six children fatherless and the
cottage by the dirt road owned by people named Coughlan
awaits us without television and the fields lead to the edge
of the water and the place where you find the sheep's skull
and Mam won't let you take it inside and it rots on the

window ledge and beneath the thatched roof Swallows and Amazons and Famous Five and Hardy Boys' mysteries mark the long days of summer until once more the Rowntree Mackintosh factory and Kilmainham Jail appear and Da declares there to be "no place like home."

A Note from the Author

I am incredibly grateful to the teachers and mentors who spurred me along the way: Kevin O'Brien, Fergal O'Doherty, Geoffrey Wolff, Jim Wilcox, James G. Bennett, Michael Bowman , and my late friend and mentor, Jeanne Leiby. My mother, Elizabeth Claffey, who instilled in me her love of literature and the theatre, and my father, Jack Claffey, a great storyteller. My brothers, Johnny, Michael, and Lorcan, who constantly encourage and support me. To Jennifer Paddock, Ronlyn Domingue, Alison Grifa, Laura Jones, Deborah Centola, Ari Gratch, and all the folks I met in Louisiana and the South who directly, or indirectly influenced my writing. To Joe De Salvo and Rosemary James of Faulker House Books for their kindness and support, and to the city of New Orleans where many of these stories had their beginnings. I owe a debt to the online literary community at Fictionaut, too numerous to mention them all here, and I'd only forget someone, and particularly to Meg Pokrass whose writing prompts gave me many a starting point. Thanks also are due to Joe and Mara O'Dwyer for their love and support, and for literally providing a safe harbor in a storm. I am deeply grateful to the editors in whose various journals and magazines my writing has appeared. Closer to home, I thank my friends and family in California, the Foleys, Bailards, Whites, David Hedges, Patrick Corrigan, Giti White, and other co-conspirators. Many thanks to Paul Bartsch for revamping my website. Thanks too, to Kevin Morgan Watson and Christine Norris of Press 53, for their diligence and patience in the editing and publication of this book. I'm grateful to my children, Simon and Maisie, for reminding me of what matters. Finally, to Maureen, who brought me back to writing after years in the wilderness.

JAMES CLAFFEY hails from County Westmeath, Ireland, and lives on an avocado ranch in Carpinteria, California, with his wife, the writer and artist, Maureen Foley, their daughter, Maisie, and occasionally his son, Simon. James' writing has appeared in numerous journals, magazines and anthologies. He is currently working on a novel based on his childhood in Ireland. His website is www.jamesclaffey.com.

Cover artist **Þorkell (Thorkell) Sigvaldason** has always been fascinated with photography. When he was younger, he would always ask to use his father's camera. After a couple of years of this, he finally got a camera as a present. He says, "It wasn't much, but it was mine." Later, after getting a digital camera, he started taking more photos and putting them online where other people might see them. He says, "I'm mostly interested in landscape photography, but I take photographs of other things as well." Regarding the cover photo, "Bird in Snow," he adds, "I shot this through a really dirty window. It's not like I could've opened something; the bird would've flown away at the slightest sound from me."

Discover more of Þorkell's photography at www.flickr.com/photos/thorkell.

CPSIA information can be obtained at www.ICGtesting.com
Printed in the USA
LVOW06s1102230714

395295LV00003B/106/P

9 781935 708919